CHANCES ARE

PACIFIC BAY SERIES - BOOK 1

KELLIE COATES GILBERT

Copyright © 2020 by Kellie Coates Gilbert LLC

Published by Amnos Media Group

All rights reserved.

Cover design: The Killion Group

Photo image: Jasmine Chen, Vancouver B.C.

No part of this book may be reproduced in any form or by any electronic or mechanical means, including information storage and retrieval systems, without written permission from the author, except for the use of brief quotations in a book review.

www.kelliecoatesgilbert.com

This book is dedicated to David Roper, Brett Meador and Matt Reynolds - gifted teachers who have greatly blessed me.

WHAT OTHERS ARE SAYING ABOUT KELLIE'S BOOKS...

"Well-drawn, sympathetic characters and graceful language"
  ~**Library Journal**

"Deft, crisp storytelling"
  ~**RT Book Reviews**

"I devoured the book in one sitting."
  ~**Chick Lit Central**

"Gilbert's heartfelt fiction is always a pleasure to read."
  ~**Buzzing About Books**

ALSO BY KELLIE COATES GILBERT

THE PACIFIC BAY SERIES

Chances Are

Remember Us

Chasing Wind

Between Rains

THE SUN VALLEY SERIES

Sisters

Heartbeats

Changes

Promises

LOVE ON VACATION SERIES

Otherwise Engaged

All Fore Love

TEXAS GOLD SERIES

A Woman of Fortune

Where Rivers Part

A Reason to Stay

What Matters Most

CHANCES ARE
PACIFIC BAY SERIES, BOOK 1

Kellie Coates Gilbert

1

Allie Barrett's hands gripped the steering wheel a little tighter as her car headlights lit up the winding two-lane blacktop lined with ferns and canopied by spruce. She rolled down her window. Instantly, the air inside her 1998 Chevy Blazer filled with the scent of pine and salt air, signaling she must be nearing the coast.

She glanced in the rearview mirror at the sleeping boy in the back seat and smiled. Her son needed the sleep. It'd been a long trip.

Ahead, a sign appeared alongside the road saying she had less than a hundred miles to her destination. Feeling a mixture of anticipation and nerves, she fiddled with the radio knob. Unable to tune into a station that didn't crackle, she finally gave up and hummed a favorite Taylor Swift tune about starting over, her new life theme.

She held that thought as doubts sprouted, hoping she hadn't made the wrong decision. She couldn't start a new life if she kept trying to hold onto the old one. Did she want to live a half of a life?

No—she wanted the whole shebang. Even if this move was scary.

With her full attention directed on the road, she rounded a tight bend and squinted against the darkness. The car engine made a knocking noise as the road headed into a sharp incline. Allie pressed the gas pedal down and hoped for the best. The last thing she needed was car trouble.

Her old Chevy Blazer had made it over the past three thousand plus miles without incident, a real feat for a vehicle with over one hundred and fifty thousand miles on its odometer and a paint job that had seen much better days.

Until this past week, she'd never ventured out of Texas. Few would have imagined she'd have the guts to pack up Ryan and head to Oregon, least of all her ex-husband—bless his wandering heart.

It hadn't been easy, living as a single mother. While she'd been on her own for most of their marriage, living without Deacon Ray was still an adjustment, even after nearly two years. She often felt like an armadillo waddling the side of the road about to get smashed by a wayward tire.

So, when that letter arrived from Oregon . . . Well, the way she figured it, that letter was the hand of God presenting her with the opportunity to start over, a chance to create a new life for Ryan and herself. Oh sure, a surprise inheritance was like a plot out of those romance novels her mama used to read, but she didn't care. She'd take it.

She desperately needed a new life.

Allie had never met her benefactor, but her mama spoke of her uncle often. She was so proud of her little brother and all he'd built. "He has a fishing boat out there, Allie. Made it big for a kid from Ding Dong."

Yes, there really was a town in Texas called Ding Dong.

Her hometown, located about an hour north of Austin, was founded in the 1930s by a couple named Zelis and Burt Bell, who owned a store in town. One day, they hired a painter to paint their store sign. A local jokester convinced the painter to paint two bells on the sign and label them Zelis and Burt after the couple, and then write under the bells, "Ding Dong." The painter took the advice and the town was known as Ding Dong ever since.

Today, the tee-niny town had dwindled to near non-existence—only had a couple dozen homes, a café on Main Street, one tiny Southern Baptist church where her daddy used to pastor and a volunteer fire department made up of three old men well into their retirement. Men who could barely lift a firehose, let alone climb a ladder.

Truth was, she hadn't been back to Ding Dong in ages. Not since moving to Dallas with Deacon Ray the year after Mama died. At the time, she'd been pregnant and filled with hope. Of course, that hadn't all turned out as she'd wanted.

At the hillcrest, a deer stood motionless and alert in a clearing alongside the road, a little fawn by her side. As the headlights neared, the doe and its baby bolted into a thick stand of pines.

She glanced at her watch. Two o'clock a.m. Her destination was still over an hour away.

Perhaps she should have stayed in Portland for the night, but her meager budget wouldn't allow for the cost of an extra night in a hotel. While the drive south on Interstate 5 had been an easy drive, she hadn't counted on how this leg of I-20 heading west to the coast, with its long and winding roadway through the Cascade mountain range, would slow her progress.

A loud pop rang out, followed by a raucous *thapping* sound as rubber slapped against pavement.

Allie groaned out loud and gripped the steering wheel tightly to keep the car from veering off-road.

A flat tire—that's all she needed!

Ryan's head bolted up from the backseat. "Mom?" He rubbed at his eyes. "What's that noise?"

"Shhh...go back to sleep, baby. It's just a flat tire. I'll have it fixed in no time. Really, lie down and go back to sleep."

"But you might need help—"

"No, baby. I got it. Go back to sleep." Allie eased the vehicle onto a wide spot in the road and pulled to a stop, turned on her emergency flashers.

She sighed as she glanced out the window at the steep hillside covered with thick pine trees. She'd lost cell service miles back.

Undeterred, she reached over the front seat to the glove box and pulled out a flashlight and a pair of gloves before she stepped into the pitch-black darkness. It'd been over an hour since she'd seen another car, which wasn't necessarily a bad thing. The scene outside would have made the perfect setting for a slasher movie.

Before her mind could take off in wild places, Allie stubbornly yanked the gloves onto her hands and used the dim flashlight to make her way to the back of the car. The tire was a goner.

After surveying the damage, she carefully pulled open the rear hatch door.

Straddling the trailer hitch to the U-Haul, Allie unloaded the tightly packed contents from the Blazer's rear compartment onto the road so she could gain access to where the spare was stored.

A bank of fog broke overhead. Moonlight shone through the misty forest providing much-needed light for the task ahead. She pulled the dusty tire from the cargo area and dropped it onto the loamy soil lining the pavement. The tire bounced a couple of times before falling on its side, making a circling motion and finally coming to a rest.

Well, let's see if I remember how to do this.

Allie brushed the dirt from her gloved hands and reached for the jack kit. She laid the tools onto the pavement and said a little prayer as she kicked the spare tire forward and dropped down on one knee to loosen the lug nuts on the rim, remembering when she and her mama had a flat tire on their way to church years ago.

"C'mon, Allie girl. We've got a tire to fix," her mama said, climbing out of their old Pontiac.

"Why don't we go knock on Mr. Pearson's door and see if he'll help us?"

Her mama shook her head vehemently. "The good Lord helps those who help themselves. Besides, a twelve-year-old should know how to change a tire. Now get on over here close and I'll show you how."

Allie smiled at the memory as she reached for the tire iron. Once she'd popped off the hub cap, she picked up the lug wrench and attempted to loosen the lug nuts. Unfortunately, they wouldn't budge.

A sound interrupted the darkness. Her skin prickled. It was the sound of someone—or something—walking across broken branches.

She swallowed.

Probably another deer, she told herself as she forced her way to a large stone at the edge of the road, determined not to let silly fear get the better of her. She wedged the flashlight between her armpit and forearm, then leaned and picked the heavy rock up before nervously glancing around at the shadows satisfied the large stone had two uses, if necessary.

She lugged the rock back to the car and used the bulky heft to knock against the dangling lug wrench. Once—bam! Twice—bam!

Third time's a charm.

Allie held her breath and slammed the rock harder this

time. She felt the lug give way. She exhaled, feeling immense relief. "That should do it."

Minutes later, she had the tire replaced and the flat stored back in place. Satisfied, she went to work and repacked their belongings, including a nearly empty cooler she'd filled with food so they didn't have to stop and spend money on the trip. In a moment of weakness, she'd given in to Ryan's pleas for a treat and pulled in to a Burgerville drive-in while driving through Portland. They splurged on an order of big ole Walla Walla sweet onion rings and a shared milkshake, even though that hazelnut shake cost a whopping four dollars.

Her stomach growled. That stop had been hours ago.

Putting mind over matter, Allie stifled a yawn and slid back into the front seat of her car where the deed to her recently deceased uncle's house and title to his fishing boat were tucked securely inside her bag, right next to her divorce papers.

Allie tried like crazy to hold on to her marriage, but there were just so many times she could forgive after coming home to find some girl in her bed. A gal had her dignity, you know?

Those two years since their split had been hard ones, especially for Ryan. As time went on, his dad reached out less and less. Despite shared custody, he seemed to always have excuses for why he couldn't keep Ryan for the weekend or his holidays.

Then Deacon Ray got a wild hair and took off out-of-state for a job months ago. She'd heard through the grapevine he had a gal with him. Except for a Christmas card months ago, they hadn't heard from him since.

She checked the backseat. Despite all the noise she'd been making, Ryan was still sound asleep.

That was the most difficult thing in all of this—trying to help her little boy understand how life could be sometimes.

But, like her mama always said, "When things take a turn for the worse, simply flip the page. Chances are, you never know what story might be in the very next chapter."

She breathed in deeply, let the heady smell of that Oregon air coming in from the open car window clear her head.

She was doing exactly that—stepping into the next chapter. There were lots of reasons to be apprehensive, but life could still deliver a happily ever after ending.

Feeling more than ready to get back on the road, she eased the car back onto the narrow two-lane highway.

Fighting to stay awake, Allie drove the final miles of her long journey in silence until she rounded a wide bend in the road where a large sign lit by floodlights at the base came into view. A lighthouse and a whale were carved in the middle with large gold lettering that read: *Welcome to Pacific Bay. Oregon's friendliest town.*

A buzzy feeling ran down her back. With a trace of a smile, she gripped the steering wheel and focused on the town that lay ahead, relishing the faint apricot-colored morning dawning over the misty rooftops.

This was their new chapter. She couldn't wait for the story to unfold.

2

"Ryan, honey. Wake up!" Allie reached over the back seat and shook her sleeping boy. "Ryan, baby. You've got to see this!"

Upon entering town, she'd followed the signs and driven straight to the beach. For nearly ten minutes, she'd sat in silent awe, taking in the expanse of water, the waves and sand, the roaring sound. Now, she couldn't wait another minute to share all of this with her boy.

Ryan raised his head slowly, rubbed his eyes. "Are we here?"

"Yes, baby. We're here. And look! The ocean, Ryan. Baby, it's amazing!" She jumped from the car and opened the rear door, pulled at his arm. "C'mon, let's go."

His eyes widened. "Oh, wow! Look how big it is."

"I know, right?" She grabbed his hand. With her other hand, she tugged off her shoes and socks dropping them onto the hardened wet sand. Ryan did the same while running to keep up with her.

At the water's edge, they stopped and grinned at each other. "Ready?"

Ryan nodded. "Ready."

They burst forth, running into the surf with abandon. Almost as quickly, they came to a dead stop. The water was ice cold. Freezing, in fact.

Allie started to back away from the frothy water's edge. Ryan pulled at her arm. "No, c'mon. It's the ocean, Mom."

Allie threw her head back, breathed in the smell of brackish air. "Yes, the ocean. Let's go."

Despite the frigid water temps, they ran through the swells that broke and crept across their feet—laughing with abandon.

Several feet away, a man in a parka walked a black Labrador on a leash. He sipped from a Starbucks cup. He waved as he passed, seeming to enjoy their antics.

Allie waved back, then bent to pick up a perfectly shaped sand dollar. "Ryan, look at this."

"I know, Mom. They're all over the beach. And look at that jelly-like stuff. What's that?"

"Jellyfish, I would suppose," she told him, her feet now aching from the cold. "Did you see the lighthouse?" She pointed.

"I know, cool. Just like in the pictures."

"As fun as this is, my feet are aching from the cold and I'm starving. What do you say we head back to the car and dry off, then head for some breakfast? We have a big day ahead of us."

He moaned. "Do we have to?"

"Do I need to remind you we live here now? We can come back. As often as we like."

Ryan's face brightened. "Yeah. We live here now." He paused, looked at her with a pensive expression. "Mom?"

"Yeah?"

"Where exactly do we live?"

She gave him a reassuring smile, put her arm around his shoulders. "Let's have breakfast and then we'll go find out." She reached out and tried to smooth down Ryan's hair, but it couldn't be done. It was a minefield of cowlicks. He needed a haircut and she'd get him one as soon as she landed a job.

The small coastal community of Pacific Bay was everything she'd dreamed. It was so picturesque, just like in the images on the internet.

Craggy cliffsides hugged the shoreline in places, with glass-fronted homes perched on top sporting decks that granted the lucky owners million-dollar views. Below, clusters of houses with gray-weathered siding and white-paned windows lined narrow roadways bordered with picket fences.

Flowers brightened the scene. Deep-blue hydrangeas, climbing rosebushes bursting with pink blooms and proud foxgloves standing tall among happy-faced daisies swaying in the gentle ocean breezes.

Deeper in town, shops of every sort lined Main Street. Antique shops, gift shops, and stores offering cotton candy and saltwater taffy in hundreds of flavors—at least that's what the brightly colored signs in the windows promised.

Hanging pots cascading with red geraniums, blue lobelia, and pink petunias lined the streets. Some shops were painted with murals featuring whales and ocean scenes. And there was a street-side window giving tourists a peek into a busy fish cannery.

Allie pulled onto a street bordering the harbor. In the distance, a long bridge spanned the entry to the Pacific. Gray-shingled rental cottages dotted the edge of a long pier where every kind of sea vessel imaginable filled the boat slips—crabbing boats, fishing boats, whale-watching rigs. Everything was just like described in the travel guide she'd secretly ordered when considering the move.

More importantly, somewhere down there was the house that would be their new home. She couldn't wait to make her way to the address included in the letter from her deceased uncle's lawyer. But first things first.

She pulled into an empty parking spot along Main Street. "We should be able to find something here." She put the car in park and killed the ignition. "You hungry, buddy?"

"Starving," Ryan answered, unhooking his seat belt.

Even at this early hour, the area was already bustling with people anxious to visit the art galleries and restaurants along the wharf. Allie linked arms with her son and together they made their way to the front door of a quaint little place with faded pink shutters and window boxes filled with flowers. A sign above the door read Pig 'n' Pancake.

"Mmm... I smell bacon." She grabbed for the doorknob.

Inside, tables covered with red-and-white-checked oilcloth lined the windows. The tables were all full, so she placed her hands on Ryan's shoulders and pointed him to the counter located near the front window next to the cash register. It was lined with swivel bar stools. "Let's sit here."

Ryan slid into one of the red vinyl banquette seats, then grabbed a worn plastic-covered menu from a little silver rack on the counter. "Are we sharing?" he asked, scanning the items and their prices.

"Not this time. I'm too hungry."

"Can I have some of these huckleberry pancakes?" he asked. "Uh, what are huckleberries anyway?"

A man who looked to be in his late sixties stepped to the counter in front of them. He wore jeans and an unbuttoned plaid flannel shirt over a striped T-shirt. He was so skinny he'd have to stand twice to make a shadow. The hair that remained on his balding head was gray and worn long and a bit scraggly.

"Those tiny berries are the best thing your mouth will ever taste," he announced, pulling a mug from the shelf and holding it in front of her. "Cup of joe?"

Allie nodded. "Yes, please."

He set the mug down in front of her. "Huckleberries are only found in the mountainous regions of the Pacific Northwest." He turned and grabbed a clear glass carafe off a hotplate before filling her cup to the brim. "Cream?"

She shook her head. "No, thanks."

"Anyways," he continued. "Huckleberries are indigenous to Oregon and are delicious to the palate. I strongly recommend you try some."

Ryan lifted his eyebrows in consideration. "Thank you, sir. I think I will." He closed his menu and handed it off to the man. "And some bacon too." He looked to his mom. "If it's not too much."

Allie grinned. "We're good." She closed her menu. "I'll have a ham and swiss omelet."

"Another excellent choice," the man said, grinning. His craggy face reminded her of the Maritime maps hanging on the walls of the restaurant, full of many lines and markings but simple to read and follow, she supposed, if a person made the effort. And he certainly seemed to know his plant trivia.

"The cheese is from the Tillamook Cheese Factory just up the road north of here," the man added. "A place well worth touring."

Ryan swung back and forth in the bar stool. "Oh, we're not tourists. We live here."

The old man eyed them. "I know just about every person who calls Pacific Bay home. Don't think I've seen you around."

Allie tucked a stray piece of hair behind her ear. "Just arrived. In fact, maybe you can give me some directions. The app on my phone doesn't seem to be able to locate this address." She dug in her bag and pulled out the letter, handed it to him.

"Oh, you're Tarver McIntosh's niece from Texas."

Allie raised her brows. "You know me?"

"I know of you. Tarver was a friend. Hated that he spent his last months in Portland in the Veteran's Administration hospital. I visited him as often as I could get over that way. He told me of his plans to leave his place and boat to his sister's kid. I take it that must be you."

"Yes," she confirmed. "I'm afraid I never had the pleasure of meeting my uncle."

The man scribbled on a little tablet, tore the sheet out and secured it to the silver rack hanging from the window-like opening to the kitchen. He gave the rack a slight spin and hollered, "Order up."

He turned his gaze back their way. "Well, it's not always easy for families to stay connected when they live so far away." He wiped his leathery hands on a bar towel hanging from the ties on his apron, then extended a hand. "I'm Muncy Davis. This here is my place. Actually, me and my boy's. Welcome to town."

Allie shook his hand. "Nice to meet you. I'm Allie Barrett and this is my son, Ryan."

"Pleasure to meet you, young man."

A shy smile nipped at the corners of Ryan's mouth. "Same here, sir."

The guy winked. "Friends call me Muncy."

Allie smiled over at her soon-to-be eleven-year-old son. He was such a polite kid. So many moms complained about their kids, claimed they were unruly and smart-mouthed. Not Ryan. He was a real treasure. And she wasn't just saying that because she was his mom.

Muncy handed the letter back to her. "Tarver's old place is down on the harbor." He took out a napkin and drew a crude map, marking her destination with an X. "Can't miss it," he told her. "But be prepared. Tarver let the place run down a little while he was sick. We all tried to help out but he was a stubborn ole cuss and claimed he wasn't a charity case."

Allie smiled. "Sounds like my mama and her brother were a lot alike."

Minutes later, Muncy returned and slid platters of steaming hot food onto the counters in front of them. "Enjoy," he said.

The breakfast was delicious. The omelet was brimming with chopped ham and oozing cheese and came with a side of sourdough toast and blackberry jam. Ryan's pancakes were the size of the bottom of her mama's old frypan, dotted with dark purple berries, with bacon mounded up high on the side of the plate.

They were hungry and she had to remind Ryan not to gobble his food. When they'd finished, she fished her wallet out of her bag.

Muncy appeared yet again and held up his hands. "This one's on me. A welcome gift, so to speak. And a nod to my friend, Tarver."

Allie shook her head vehemently. "No, I'm happy to pay."

He covered her hand with his own, looked her straight in the eyes. "I insist."

Allie relented, summoned her most charming smile. "Well, I suppose. Just this once. And thank you so much."

"No problem." He gazed back at her, hesitated. "Say, what are you going to be doing for work?"

Ryan piped up. "Oh, she needs a job. And she's going to get one. Just as soon as we get settled."

"Well, I'm not sure what you're looking for, but as you can see, this place is hopping during the summer tourist season. Sometimes, people are lined up outside the door and down the sidewalk waiting to get in. One of my regular gals is out on medical leave. I could use some help to fill in for a few weeks until she gets back." The old man shrugged. "And you're under no obligation. The job's temporary. If you find something more suitable, you're free to move on. Not a second thought about it." He looked at her, waited.

Allie couldn't believe her ears. It was as if the hand of God had reached down and asked her to dance or something. "A job? Here?" She grinned. "Why, that would be wonderful!"

Muncy clapped his veined hands together. "Then it's

settled. You get on over to your uncle's house and get moved in. Then you can start. Say, a week from Monday?"

Her heart raced with pure relief. "Absolutely. Monday, it is. And thank you, Mr. Davis."

"Remember, my friends call me Muncy." He winked.

She nodded, gave him a sheepish smile. "Of course. Muncy."

Outside, the gray-dappled sky had turned sunny and bright. She grabbed Ryan's hand and pulled him to the car, laughing out loud. "See that, Ryan? Everything's going to turn out. I mean, I had my reservations. I didn't want to admit it. I'm just as scared about all this change as anyone would be. But things are just falling into place. I think we're going to be really happy here."

"Do you think Dad is happy too? I mean, wherever he is?"

The unexpected question stabbed Allie's heart. She reached for the car door handle, glanced over at the boy she loved more than life itself, and swallowed. "Yes, baby. I'm pretty sure he is."

3

Her uncle's house was nothing she expected.

"Wow, Mom. This is pretty bad," Ryan said, staring at their new home as he slowly climbed from the car.

Allie stood there trying to take it all in. The house was more the size of a cottage, the kind you might see filled with elves in a Disney movie. Weather-worn shakes covered the outer walls. Shutters in bad need of paint hung at paned windows with window boxes filled with weeds. A rusted-out bicycle leaned against the wall to the right of the front door.

The only pretty thing was a bunch of bright-blue hydrangeas growing at the edge of the deck leading to the door —that, and a pair of yellow butterflies staggering among a cluster of daylilies, drunk with nectar.

Allie swallowed and forced a bright tone. "Oh, it's not so awful." She stepped onto the creaking deck. "Just needs a little elbow grease, that's all."

Ryan looked doubtful. "And some ankle grease, wrist grease and bacon grease."

She ruffled his hair. "Lucky for us we have all that," she

said, trying to bring a smile to his face. "We just need to get busy. You and I will roll up our sleeves, get to work and have everything in shape in no time."

Allie dug in her purse and pulled out the key the lawyer had sent with the letter. She stepped to the front door, surprised to find it slightly open. She maneuvered the key into the lock to make sure it worked. It did. At least they'd be able to secure the door at night while they slept.

She slowly eased the door open and stepped inside. The house was dark and smelled dank and musty. Sheets hung over the windows and over all the furniture. Her eyes had a hard time adjusting to the darkened interior.

Ryan followed close behind. He flicked the light switch and the room they were standing in lit up. "Well, at least we have electricity."

Allie glanced around, speechless.

The interior was worse than she'd ever pictured in her mind, much worse. Everything was covered with dust, and not just a little. A person could grow carrots in the layer on the flooring.

Ryan plunged his hands in his pockets. "Gross."

She more than agreed. Still, she was determined to be upbeat. "Oh, now. Come on. This is nothing a little soap and water won't fix. I promise, by this time next week, you won't even remember what we walked into." She glanced over at her son, hoping her attitude might erase the look on his dejected face. "When have the two of us ever been unable to turn sour apples into pie?"

"I dunno, Mom. This is... Well, it's really dirty."

While not admitting the fact out loud, Allie couldn't argue. Their new start was already facing some challenges. No matter what, it was her job to teach Ryan to look at the bright side, despite how hard things got.

She gave his shoulder a slight shove. "Race you. First one to the U-Haul gets their choice of ice cream at that little shop we passed this morning. The sign said they had twenty-four flavors to choose from."

Before he could answer, she forced a laugh, turned and bolted back out the door.

He hesitated only briefly before following in a dead run.

They spent the following hours unloading boxes, stacking them against the wall to be unpacked later. Together, they juggled what few furniture items had fit in the tiny cargo trailer into the house. The mattress and box springs proved the most difficult. They heaved and pulled on the unwieldy items until they had them in place on a bed frame and squeaky set of bedsprings in the bedroom, one of the sparse items her uncle had left behind.

Thankfully, he also left an upholstered sofa and chair. Both had holes repaired with duct tape. They required a good vacuuming, but they'd do for now.

Her uncle's cupboards were nearly bare except for a few canned food items. She tossed them all in the garbage, took out a bucket and filled it with the hottest water her hands could stand. Then she poured some bleach in, and scrubbed those shelves until her knuckles were raw.

Ryan was a huge help. He swept and took a mop to the wood floors. Once cleaned of the grime, they didn't look too bad.

They scrubbed the toilet best they could, wiped down mirrors and scoured the tub. When they'd finished most of the cleaning chores, they got busy and unpacked the few clothes they had in their suitcases and hung them in the closet using black wire hangers her uncle left behind.

The refrigerator took the longest. Allie had to take out a screwdriver and tinker with the motor at the back to get the thing running again. Thank goodness for YouTube videos and an unlocked internet connection from the nearby marina.

By the time darkness fell, both Ryan and Allie agreed they were far too tired to head for ice cream, or even dinner, for that matter.

"Raincheck?" Allie asked. They'd finish up what food they had in the cooler. And there were two Twinkies left.

Ryan nodded and unbuttoned his shirt. "Yeah, I just want to go to bed."

Allie swallowed the tiny wave of sadness that swept over her. An eleven-year-old should be out playing ball, not spending ten hours scrubbing and mopping.

"Hey," she told him, taking his shirt and flipping it over her shoulder to hang up later. "What say tomorrow we tackle the outside of this place for a couple of hours, then take a break and go exploring?"

His face brightened, but only slightly. "Sure."

Allie opened her cooler, pulled out the last of the potato salad. She forgot they ate up the package of lunch meat and cheese the day before. She grabbed two forks, handed Ryan one. "C'mon, let's eat and then get some sleep. It's been a long day."

"Mom, are one of those boats down at the marina ours?"

Allie peered out the kitchen window. The glow from the setting sun played off the placid surface of the water, giving the bay a golden hue. "That's what the letter said. We'll go check it out tomorrow."

"And can I learn to drive it? When I get big enough, I mean?"

She grinned at him. "When you're big enough, you can learn to take her out on fishing excursions. We have a lot to learn, you and me. But life's an adventure—and this is going to be one of the biggest."

He smiled at that and dug back into the container of potato salad.

A short time later, they finished their scant dinner and headed for bed.

"Sorry you don't have your own bed, Ryan. Until we can get you one, I'll sleep on the sofa." She grabbed a folded sheet from the box at the foot of the bed.

"Mom?"

"Yeah?"

"Could you—I mean, I don't mind if you sleep with me tonight."

Allie nodded. Yes, he was eleven, but everything was new, and frankly, she'd sleep better by his side too. "Really?" she said. "Because I was a little nervous sleeping by myself for the first night. But I didn't want to impose."

He grinned. "It's okay, Mom. Sleep here."

It didn't take long for both of them to conk out. Allie was in a dead sleep, dreaming about the ocean, when a noise pulled her awake.

Her eyes popped wide open. She tried to gain her bearings, then remembered where she was.

"Mom? What was that?" Ryan whispered. She could hear the fear in his voice.

Taking a steadying breath, she used her best *I got this handled* voice. "Nothing, babe. Go back to sleep."

He did as he was told, cuddled closer.

Then she heard it again.

A noise—louder this time. A scurrying of little feet.

There was an animal in the bedroom!

She sat straight up at the same time Ryan grabbed her arm. She flipped her phone flashlight feature on and pointed it around the room. A beam of light landed on two pairs of eyes staring back at her from the floor across the room.

She couldn't help it. She screamed.

Ryan screamed.

The beady eyes, and the legs that went with them, raced across the room and made a beeline for the open closet door.

Allie swallowed. "It's okay, Ryan. It's just a small animal of some sort." She reached and flipped on the bedside lamp, praying it wasn't a skunk. "Stay here," she told him, climbing from the bed. She pulled her jeans on under her nightgown, then slid her feet into her sneakers and carefully trod across the floor with the laces untied.

She paused at the closet door, unwilling to show her building panic. She knew Ryan was watching.

"Mom, take the broom!"

Her head bobbed in an enthusiastic nod. "Yeah, good idea."

Minutes later, bristled weapon in hand, she ventured back to the closet. Using her foot, she kicked at Ryan's shoes, then the tiny suitcase stored on the floor of the closet.

That's all it took.

A big rat, nearly the size of a small dog, followed by what must've been his wife, barreled out of the closet. They ran right over the top of her sneakers and bolted under the bed. She screamed and jumped back.

Ryan stood on top of the bed, the sheets tucked tightly under his chin. "Now what?"

Allie took another deep breath. She couldn't just leave the varmints under their bed—not if they wanted to get a wink of shuteye.

She stopped and considered her options, landing on one that might just work. "Ryan, come help me."

"No! I'm not getting down off the bed. Not with those things down there."

She relented. "Okay. I can do it. Just keep an eye open for me. Let me know if they move."

She proceeded to collect empty boxes from the stacks by the wall and lined them from the bedroom door to the front door, now glad the house had such a small footprint. When finished, there was an inescapable path, or at least she hoped so.

Still feeling shaky inside, she opened the front door and returned to the bedroom.

This time, she took boxes and fenced in the entire circumference of the bed, a corral of sorts, leaving one opening and created a boxed-in-pathway to the one at the bedroom door where Ryan was huddled up on the bed against the wall, trying his best to be brave.

There were few occasions where she really wished she had a man by her side, any man. Maybe even the one she'd divorced. Now was one of those times.

She pushed the thought from her mind, slowly lowered to her knees, praying that her plan would work and there would be no opportunity for those rats to escape beyond the route she'd devised—and especially no wayward rats running up her nightgown.

She shuddered and told herself that would never happen. Not entirely convinced, she grabbed the broom, slid it between the small space between two boxes, and quickly fanned the handle back and forth in a sweeping motion under the bed.

Thunk!

She hit one.

As hoped, the uninvited guests bolted out and down the escape route she'd built with a second right behind, their furry bodies nearly a blur as they raced out, with long, nasty tails trailing behind.

Allie ran after them, watching as they jumped out the open door and into the darkness.

Relieved, she leaned the broom against the wall and moved to shut the front door, quickly locking it. She brushed her open palms against each other, dusting off the dirt and her earlier fear. "And don't come back," she said, for good measure.

She moved the boxes and stacked them back up. A half-hour later, she finally returned to bed.

Ryan was sound asleep, nestled with the covers wrapped around his legs. He had a peaceful look on his face—the same expression she'd stared at for hours on end when he was a baby napping in his crib.

Rare tears sprouted. A lump grew in her throat.

"Oh, Ryan. If you only knew how much your mama loves you," she whispered, climbing in next to him. She brushed a sweaty strand of hair from his face, leaned in and kissed his forehead. "I vow to do everything in my power to make things different. To give you the life you deserve."

Her hand swept away an uninvited tear trailing down her cheek. She reached and turned off the lamp.

"I promise."

4

Morning dawned early with sounds from the marina waking Allie, sounds foreign to a girl from Texas. Foghorns and seagulls cawing. Rumbling boat engines idling in the distance.

She climbed from the bed, leaving her boy sleeping. After scrounging in a box for her coffee maker, she brewed a pot, grabbed her steaming mug and headed outdoors to check out the source of those sounds, and her new surroundings.

At the base of the pier across the water, a chorus of large black seals barked their strange sound, first one and then the others. The sound reminded her of old Mrs. Otis back in Ding Dong that time she got bronchitis and came to church coughing her silly head off.

At the other end of the pier, men in orange overalls and black boots loaded the decks of their boats with crabbing rings, their voices echoing from across the small bay. Not far from where she stood, she could hear water lapping against the rocks as a boat wake drifted across the water to the bay's edge.

The boats docked in the marina were too numerous to count, their masts standing tall against blue sky shining above a line of pines in the far distance. The scene looked like something right out of a movie.

As tired as she was, she took it all in, relishing the sights and sounds. Until now, she'd only experienced the coastal experience on the internet. Everything was far more extraordinary in person.

Take, for instance, the way the sky was filled with cotton-candy-pink tinged clouds—a sign the day was going to be a pretty one.

She wondered why her mama had never brought her here for a visit. Of course, a trip of that distance was not likely feasible for their limited family budget. Still, who knew such beauty existed? Certainly, not this girl from Texas.

Allie took a sip of her coffee, smiled as another foghorn sounded. She was blessed to experience the extraordinary sights and sounds now, and to be able to expose Ryan to all of this. Even if the experience included a tangle with rats.

"Hey, Mom. What you doing out here?"

She looked over to see Ryan standing in his pajamas, his hair standing on end.

"Hey, there." She motioned. "Come over here and join me."

He gave her a goofy grin. "I dreamed I was Christopher Columbus last night."

"You did, huh?" She ruffled his hair and pulled him into a tight hug, resting her chin on top of his head. "Well, Mr. Columbus. What say you get dressed and we go grab some breakfast and then go exploring? We need to discover a grocery store."

"Yeah," he said with excitement. "We can finish our chores later. Besides, you owe me some ice cream."

She smiled. "Yes, I sure do."

After a brief discussion, they decided to hit the Pig 'n' Pancake again. A bell inside the tiny restaurant tinkled when they opened the door.

Muncy waved from behind the counter. "Well, there's our new friends. How'd the first night in your new place go?"

Ryan slid into a barstool. "It was filthy! We worked like dogs all day to clean the place up."

Allie hid her slight embarrassment. "It wasn't that bad."

"Yes, it was," Ryan argued. "And the whole place smelled. But we got everything put in order. Well, almost."

Muncy grinned, wiped his hands on the towel tucked inside the strings of his apron. "I bet you're both hungry. We have a special running this morning—biscuits and sausage gravy with scones and honey on the side. Comes with a glass of juice and coffee."

Allie slid onto the empty seat next to Ryan. "We'll take two orders."

Muncy nodded. "Good choice. We'll have that right up for you."

A man sitting at the end of the counter lowered the newspaper he'd been reading, gave them a sidelong look. "So, did I hear you're new to town?"

Ryan swung his barstool back and forth. "Yeah. We got here yesterday. We drove all the way from Dallas, Texas," he announced proudly.

Allie placed her hand on his knee. "Okay, Mr. Radio Station. That's probably more news than the nice man wanted to know."

His eyes twinkled. "Welcome to town."

"Thanks," she said, sizing him up.

She'd guess him to be in his late forties. He wasn't bad looking, for a man his age. Just the opposite, in fact.

His face was tanned, like he spent a lot of time outside. His light brown hair, while neatly trimmed, had a careless look and was slightly graying at the temples. He had a mustache and a cropped beard, meticulously trimmed. And gray-green eyes that seemed to see things others missed.

In fact, he looked remarkably like Kevin Costner.

Muncy reappeared with plates of hot food balanced on his forearm. He slid them onto the counter with practiced precision. "There you go. Eat up!"

He nodded to the end of the counter. "I see you've met my son."

"We didn't actually meet. At least, not officially."

Muncy's son got up and moved toward them, his hand extended. "Cameron Davis. Locals call me Cam."

Allie smiled at him, shook his hand. "Allie Barrett. And this is my son, Ryan."

Ryan stood and shook his hand. "Nice to meet you, sir," he said, before returning to his seat. He grabbed his fork and scooped a big bite into his mouth. "Mmm...this is good, Muncy!"

Muncy's face broke into a wide grin. "If you think that's good, try one of these." He reached in a glass display case and pulled out one of the largest cinnamon rolls she'd ever seen, dripping with a thick layer of frosting.

Ryan's eyes went wide. "Are you serious?"

He grinned and slid the plate in front of her son. "Here you go. Eat what you can, and I'll box the rest up for you." He turned to Allie. "On the house."

She grabbed her bag. "No, I can pay," she said in protest.

Muncy waved her off. "Your money's no good here. Consider it a sign-on bonus."

Still chewing, Ryan looked over at Cam. "My mom's going to work here."

"Temporarily," she clarified. "Only for couple of weeks. And, Ryan baby—don't talk with your mouth full."

Muncy nodded. "She's covering for Betty," he told his son.

"Ah..." Cam looked at her full-on. "So, you're Tarver's niece." He said it as more of a statement than a question.

"That's right," she said slowly.

He let out an amused laugh when he saw the look on her face. "Sorry, we get a lot of tourists that come and go, but anyone who moves to Pacific Bay? Well, that elicits a bit of discussion over coffee."

Muncy winked. "And those boys down at Search and Rescue chatter more than most."

Cameron gave his dad a look, a blush creeping up his neck. "That's not entirely true." He shifted onto his feet. "The boys down at SAR pick up a lot over the radio," he explained, though not that convincingly. Even Ryan raised his eyebrows.

"And people drop in. They talk," Cam quickly added.

"I understand. I grew up in a small town."

"You know what they say." He gazed at her warmly. "The nice part of living in a small town is that when you don't know what you're doing, everyone else does." He chuckled, then turned to Ryan. "Maybe you'd like to come over, and I'll give you a little tour of the Search and Rescue operation," he offered, clearly trying to divert the conversation. "We have a helicopter and a fleet of boats you might enjoy seeing."

Ryan dropped his fork to his plate. "A helicopter? Are you kidding? That'd be great!" He turned to Allie. "Can I, Mom. Please?"

Cam picked up his coffee mug. "You're welcome to come as well," he told her.

"Oh, I don't know. I'm going to be very busy over the coming weeks. Unpacking and all."

"Yeah, and we now own a fishing boat! We're going to get her all ready and then charge people to take them fishing."

"Is that so? On the ocean?" Cam asked, indulging her son's excitement.

"Yup! Mom says we're going to have a grand adventure."

Now it was her turn to be embarrassed. She didn't want Muncy and his son to believe she was naïve enough to think she could simply hop on a boat and drive it out into the Pacific loaded with tourists hoping to catch a salmon—but that was the end goal, eventually.

"Well, it's going to take some effort," she explained. "But yes, the letter from my uncle's attorney made it clear the boat could provide a substantial source of income."

While she didn't say so, this was another big reason she'd packed up Ryan and moved halfway across the country. She wanted Ryan to go to college and have options, which would take money. That wasn't going to happen on her meager uneducated-single-mother salary in Texas.

"Have you seen this boat?" Cam asked. "It's rumored Tarver McIntosh did fairly well but was—" He exchanged glances with his dad. "Well, he was known to be a bit eccentric."

"Not yet," she admitted. "I expect it may need some work. But I'm not opposed to putting in the labor and hiring out anything I can't do myself." She lifted her chin, privately hoping her savings would be enough. "I'll figure it out."

Muncy wiped a spot off the counter, flipped the towel over his shoulder. "Well, I admire your spirit. If there's anyone who could lend a hand, it's Cam. No one knows more about boats and the fishing industry than my son."

Cam coughed. "I'm not sure Allie's interested in all that."

A moment of silent understanding passed between father and son. Muncy grabbed the coffee carafe and refilled Allie's cup. "I'm sure my boy would be willing to help out with whatever you might need. Wouldn't you, Cameron?"

A mixture of amusement and resignation crossed Cam's face. He gave a helpless little shrug. "Sure—yeah, anything you need. But, you're right. Tarver's old boat is going to take some work. Hasn't been run in a couple of years. And there's city permits to pull and all. You can't just hang out a shingle and load up your boat with tourists."

"Which is why she's going to need our help." Muncy winked. "No one reaches the mountaintop without taking a first step up the path." He returned the carafe to the hotplate. "The great thing about living here in Pacific Bay is that no one does the hard things alone. We all gather around and offer help and whatever support we can."

Allie smiled at the sentiment. While Pacific Bay was thousands of miles from Texas, it was apparent the people could be just as neighborly.

And just like that, she knew she was home.

5

Over the following week, Allie and Ryan worked from sunup to sundown cleaning up the outside of their new home. They made a trip to the local hardware store and purchased paint, brushes and a hammer and nails. They adjusted the shutters, fastened them in place and gave each one a heavy coat of new paint.

Allie also painted the front door and window boxes and filled them with bright-red geraniums, yellow marigolds and blue lobelia she purchased from a tiny seaside nursery located ten miles north of Pacific Bay.

The deck and the steps leading up to the tiny cottage required a little more work. Her limited bank account forced her to repair what was there, even though the whole thing likely needed to be replaced. That would come later, when she got the fishing boat up and running and some much-needed revenue coming in.

Her uncle's boat, *Reel Time*, was in better shape than she'd let herself imagine, given the condition she'd found his house. Although, as Cameron Davis had suggested, her uncle was a bit eccentric. He'd painted the entire boat lavender and yellow.

Another thing Allie would immediately change when she had the money to do so.

According to the paperwork given to her by her uncle's attorney, the fifty-foot commercial vessel was built in 1976. The boat had two engines—twin 8.3 liter 400c Cummins rated at 400 horsepower each—whatever that meant. From what she could ascertain on the internet, those engines were dependable and would provide plenty of power.

Even better, the vessel was US Coast Guard certified and offshore rated out to one hundred nautical miles, was stocked with sufficient poles and equipment to take out twenty-four guests at a time and included a large holding tank for the daily catch. There was a small cabin with an oil stove and a refrigerator run by a generator.

She'd have to give the boat a good cleaning and get the licensing and permits transferred into her name, but *Reel Time* should be sufficient for what she'd need for a thriving sportfishing and whale-watching tour business.

The biggest hurdle would be getting licensed as a captain through the U.S. Coast Guard. From her online research, it looked like she'd need nearly a year of recorded sea time, pass a written exam, a drug test, and have three references. Until then, she could only be considered a skipper, meaning she'd need to hire someone who was licensed, at least initially.

All of that would cost money. Hopefully, the meager amount she'd inherited would cover her start-up expenses.

She didn't know who was more excited about this venture—her or Ryan.

"Mom, how old do I have to be before I can drive our boat?" he'd asked while standing at the helm, turning the big wheel back and forth.

She grinned and squeezed his shoulders. "You have a few years to go."

Seeing the disappointment on his face, she quickly added, "Oh, but you'll have a job. A very important job."

He looked up, excitement brimming in his eyes. "I will?"

"Oh, yes," she told him. "You will be one of our main deckhands."

He turned skeptical. "What's a deckhand?"

"Well, it's someone who helps rig and bait the lines for the guests. When a lingcod or a rockfish is caught, the deckhand helps remove the fish from the hooks. A deckhand assists the captain and the skipper in lots of ways. You think you'd be up for that?"

"Would I get paid?"

"Of course! You'd be doing a very important job." She knelt and took his face in her hands. "And I need you. Very much. This is a family business we're building. Someday, *Reel Time* will be yours."

The look of pride and satisfaction that sprouted on her son's face almost countered the churning in her gut as she thought about all the pieces that had to fall into place to meet her goals. She was a *can-do* kind of girl, never letting potential obstacles tumble her spirit—but all that faced her was a little bit daunting.

She'd bitten off a chunk here and a tiny voice inside reminded her she'd never been out to sea, never been fishing. She had a lot to learn. There was a great deal depending on her stepping up and figuring all this out, and quickly. Mainly, the bottom line in her bank account.

Which was why, later in the week, when she'd slapped the last coat of stain on the deck, she turned to Ryan. "Hey, buddy. I know we talked about heading down to the beach this afternoon, but I have a lot of things I need to do. I need to make a trip to get the boat licenses transferred over. Sorry, but you're going to have to tag along."

"Do I have to?" he complained, setting his paintbrush down on the tarp. "Sounds really boring."

"Yeah, I suppose it does," she agreed. "But, not everything in life is fun."

"Like cleaning the toilet." He scrunched his nose.

Allie laughed. "Yeah, like cleaning the toilet."

ALLIE STOOD at the front door of the U.S. Coast Guard Station, her hand on the knob. She turned to Ryan. "Now, this might take a little while. I'll need you to find a seat and be on your best behavior."

Her son rolled his eyes. "Sure."

She didn't know why she always felt the need to remind Ryan to be good. He was always polite, rarely forgetting to use his manners. Making a mental note to reward him after this meeting, she took a deep breath and prepared herself to go inside.

The Coast Guard office was located on the historic bayfront near the Pacific Bay Bridge, spanning the north jetty. The building consisted of a two-story white building with dormers, a red roof, and dark-green shutters.

Allie gave the knob a turn, eased the door open and stepped inside.

The entry was large and open with ceiling rafters which created a bit of an echo as two people wandered into an office area, talking. The floors looked to be the original wood planking, stained dark and shiny, and large, faded oil portraits hung by wires on the wall.

Across the room, a woman sat behind a large wooden desk. She looked over her reading glasses. "May I help you?"

Allie cleared her throat. "Uh, yes. Thank you." She motioned for Ryan to take a seat underneath a window overlooking the jetty. "I'm Allie Barrett. I need some help with some licensing."

The woman motioned for her to take a seat without bothering to give her name. A gold desk plaque identified her simply as *T. Vandeventer, Service Liaison.*

Over the next minutes, Allie shared all the paperwork the attorney had sent. "So, I need all the boat and the licenses transferred into my name."

"I see," the woman said, fingering the buttons on her starched white blouse. "And you plan to..."

"I hope to run the business just as my uncle did. Well, with a few changes perhaps. But—"

"I see," the woman repeated, carefully examining her uncle's license.

Allie opened her mouth to explain that the boat had been docked for over two years, but the woman held up her open palm.

Allie stopped talking, waited.

The woman scooped up all her paperwork. "Wait here." She stood and tucked the documents under her arm. Her heels made a clacking noise against the floor with every step toward a closed door.

She tapped lightly, then opened the door and stepped inside.

Allie could hear voices but couldn't make out what they were saying. She looked over at Ryan, who sat quietly, kicking his feet back and forth and looking like he would rather be cleaning those toilets he mentioned earlier.

Frankly, so would she.

It was a good ten minutes before the lady returned with her documents.

She slid into her wooden chair, looked over top her glasses. "Well, the documents all appear to be in order." She opened a desk drawer, pulled out a packet, and slid it across the desk.

"You'll have to fill all this out, in triplicate. Bring the paperwork back with a check for seven hundred and fifty dollars." She pulled out another drawer and extracted a second packet, smaller this time. "And these. This will enroll you in the mandated classwork to become eligible to apply to be a captain. Read all the safety manuals." She looked over the top of her glasses. "I suggest you read them multiple times. It's no picnic out there when a storm rolls in." She pointed out the window.

"Until then, you'll need to designate someone as captain before you take out—" She paused, glanced at the paperwork. "The *Reel Time*."

Allie took the packets, swallowed against the dryness building in her throat.

The woman lifted the documentation from the attorney and handed it over the desk as well. "Any questions?"

Allie blinked several times. "No—no, I'll look all this over."

The woman stood, her silence dismissive.

"Uh, thank you." Allie stood and motioned to Ryan. "I'll be back soon." Under her breath, she whispered, "I hope."

6
―――

On their first Saturday night in town, Allie decided they needed a treat. "Don't think I haven't noticed all you've been doing to help, Ryan. How would you like to go to a movie? The early show is half-price."

He beamed. "Can I get some popcorn too?"

She slid a can of soup into the cupboard next to the rest of the groceries she'd purchased—a package of hotdogs, milk and eggs, a box of soda crackers, two boxes of mac n' cheese, a loaf of bread and a box of Cheerios. The purchases had used up the remainder of her weekly budget.

She was stretching things with the movie tickets, so adding popcorn was out of the question.

"Afraid not, buddy." She waited for his pouty face, but none came. He was more than aware of their monetary constraints. "Oh, maybe we can go for ice cream after. Just this once."

Ryan lifted his eyebrows. "You sure, Mom? Because I can—"

"I'm sure," she assured him. "What kind of life is it if you can't have an occasional ice cream cone?"

Monday, she would start waitressing at the Pig 'n' Pancake. Even though the work would only last two weeks, she was grateful. The additional income—and hopefully some good tips—would mean she could plug a hole in her leaking bank account. It would feel good to see the balance going the other direction.

By the time the temporary job wrapped up, she hoped to use her inheritance funds and have *Reel Time* rigged and ready to go. Hopefully, that would put them on their feet financially.

There was just so much to do to make that happen. She'd spent three entire evenings hunched over the dinner table filling out all the necessary paperwork and reading the manuals.

Much of the language was foreign to her. Terms like *dock line, boddied waggler,* or *Arlesey Bomb*. And who knew that a *bird's nest* was a tangled fishing line caused by the main line coming off the spool too quickly?

The two biggest hurdles she faced were finding a captain, someone skilled and trustworthy, and getting the necessary business insurance in place. She had no idea what that might cost. She suspected the liability policy alone could whittle deeply into her savings.

She'd also discovered the need for a business license from the city of Pacific Bay. Luckily, City Hall was only a block away from Muncy's restaurant. She planned to walk over on one of her breaks next week and get that in order.

But all that could wait. Right now, she planned to spend the evening at a movie with her kid.

The movie was a cheesy Western that had released several years back, the kind you might find on a cable movie network. Even so, it felt good to get out of the house and play.

"Wasn't that cool, Mom? I mean, did you see the way that cowboy stopped those train robbers?" He shook his head. "Boy, I wish I could ride a horse like that."

Allie placed her arm casually around his shoulder and walked alongside her son while taking in the shop lights up and down the street. "What do you say you go buy that ice cream we talked about?" She stopped, dug for her wallet in her back pocket and pulled out a couple of bills, and handed them over into his waiting hand.

"What kind, Mom?"

She waved him off. "You pick. I don't want any."

Ryan frowned. "You sure?"

"I'm sure. Now, go." She pointed to a bench a few feet down the sidewalk. "I'll be waiting right there for you."

He nodded and ran off. She watched him get in line at an open window several yards away.

She turned, walked slowly to a gift shop window and peered in at the items on display. There were T-shirts, of course. And mugs with images of the iconic Pacific Bay Lighthouse. Bottles filled with shells leaned against display shelves filled with flip-flops and sun hats. Inside, the store was filled with tourists mingling the aisles.

Down the street, a line of people waited to get into Mo's Chowder House. The tantalizing aroma made her stomach rumble. She wished now she'd told Ryan to get her an ice cream.

Allie glanced in his direction, and he waved. She wiggled her fingers back at him and folded onto the bench seat to wait.

Just feet away, light spilled out an open door. Inside, she could hear one of her favorite songs—"Crazy Little Thing Called Love" by Queen. When she was little, her mother used to play the tune on the radio when they'd drive to town.

She smiled to herself and rocked to the rhythm until Ryan returned with two ice cream cones in his hands. "I could get two smalls for the price of one large," he explained and handed her one.

Allie smiled and bumped shoulders with her son. "Now, how did you know cherry chocolate chip was my favorite?"

They passed a couple standing in the doorway of another

gift shop, the girl giggling as the guy pulled her arm and they ran down the sidewalk. Allie watched as the girl leaned into him. They stopped walking, and the guy lifted her chin and kissed her.

Allie stared.

"Yuck!" Ryan said after taking a long lick off his mound of ice cream—classic strawberry, his favorite.

"What do you mean?"

Her son shrugged. "I mean, *that*." He pointed at the couple, who were still kissing.

Allie laughed. "Oh, someday you won't think kissing is yucky. I pretty much guarantee it."

Just then, the music stopped. She licked her own ice cream and watched people exiting the establishment, some of them couples holding hands and laughing.

She tried not to feel jealous. It'd been a very long time since she'd experienced anything in the romance department.

Suddenly, a familiar face appeared. Muncy's son.

He saw her too. "Hey," he said, coming over with a soda can in his hand. "What brings you two out on a night like this?"

"We went to a movie," Ryan announced. He took another lick of his ice cream.

"And I see you paid a visit to the Ice Cream Factory down the street."

Ryan nodded. "Yup. It was a treat for all the work we did this week. Huh, Mom?"

Allie couldn't help laughing a little. "Yeah. You can say that again."

Cameron placed a foot on the bench next to her, leaned over his knee. "So, you had a big week, huh?"

She nodded. "We had a bit of cleaning to do. And, that Coast Guard of yours—well, they sure don't make it easy to license a boat."

He chuckled. "No, they most certainly do not. I imagine you got an opportunity to meet Mrs. Vandeventer?"

"Who?"

"Our Service Liaison. The woman rarely smiles, and she—well, she takes her job very seriously."

Allie slowly nodded. "Oh, yes. Mrs. Vandeventer. I did have the pleasure."

"And she got you squared away?" Cam asked.

"Let's just say she loaded me down with a lot of information and paperwork."

Cam's phone buzzed. He pulled it from his pocket, checked the message, and slid it back.

"Aren't you going to get that?" Allie asked.

"Just did." He checked his watch. "Well, looks like break's about up." He drained his soda can, then looked over at Ryan. "I teach a little painting class," he explained.

Allie grew puzzled. "You paint?"

"Ah, not very well. Me and the owner of the barbershop trade off weeks and teach at the senior center." He pointed at the open door. "Dad's crowd likes to stay active, and I somehow get roped into a lot of things." He turned his attention to Ryan. "I suppose you'll be going over to the middle school next year. They have a great art program."

Ryan shuffled his feet against the sidewalk. "Yes, sir."

Cam smiled. "Well, I went there—back in the dark ages."

Allie couldn't contain her smile. "You don't look like you go back quite that far."

Cameron's eyes sparkled with amusement. "Well, looks can be deceiving. I have a grown son. He works for a law firm in Portland and is studying to take the bar exam."

A woman who looked to be in her sixties sauntered up wearing tight jeans and a shirt unbuttoned a little more than necessary. "Hey, Cam. Is your dad coming to book club on Wednesday night?"

Cam shook his head. "No, sorry. Can't this week. He's got dinner club over at Barbara Anderson's place. It's Italian night, and he's bringing the spaghetti."

The woman grinned, shrugged her shoulders. "Too bad. We're discussing John Grisham's new release. I know your dad liked his last one. Well, see you inside." She winked.

Cameron tossed his empty can into a nearby trash can.

Allie stood, tossed what remained of her melting ice cream cone in the trash as well. She nodded toward the woman walking back inside. "Looks like your father has a lot of friends."

A slow grin nipped at the corners of Cameron's mouth. "Yeah, he's pretty well booked up socially. I think he's in at least a half dozen discussion clubs. He loves to learn. Says the beautiful thing about knowledge is that no one can take it from you."

"True," she replied. "And you? What do you like to do with your evenings?'

He smiled at her and pointed over his shoulder. "Well, I do like to paint. But, I'm not nearly as social as dad. I tend to watch a little television now and then."

She shook her head. "Yeah, me too. There's nothing wrong with watching some *Wheel of Fortune*. And *Big Bang Theory* is good for the soul."

Cam made no effort to hide his amusement. "Yup, one of my favorites." He motioned for the door. "Well, looks like everybody's been to the restroom. I'd better get back." He shook Ryan's hand. "Good night, son."

"Good night, Mr. Davis."

"Friends call me Cam."

"Cam," her son repeated. "And you can call me Ryan."

That made their new friend chuckle. "Ryan it is."

He looked up at her then. "Hey, I know you start work in the morning. What say you let Ryan come over to the Coast Guard office and hang out with the guys?"

"Yeah, can I, Mom? Please?"

She grinned and nodded. "Sure, that'd be fine." She'd hated the thought of leaving him alone all day to fend for himself with nothing to do but read and watch television. "Thank you," she told Cam.

He smiled back at her. "No problem."

They watched him wander back inside. He paused and patted an old gentleman on the back and said something she couldn't make out.

Allie ruffled her son's hair. "Well, Ryan. Guess we'd better head home."

Before walking in the direction of their parked car, she couldn't help but pause at the open door where Cameron had taken his place at the front of the room. He picked up his paint brush, leaned in to the microphone. "Okay, let's take a look at how to create proportions."

Allie squeezed her son's shoulder. Together, they moved on down the sidewalk.

7

Muncy finished washing his hands in the kitchen and dried them off. "So, you ready to start?"

Allie wrapped the apron around her and tied the strings behind her back. "You bet. I'm grateful for the job."

Muncy smiled back at her. "You're doing *me* the favor." He led her to the grill. "This here's Sam Marcum. He's our cook."

Sam wiped his palms on his apron, reached out and shook hands. "I hear you're new to town. Nice to meet you."

She smiled back at the gruff-looking man with the broad, genuine smile. "Thank you. Nice to meet you as well, Sam."

Muncy pointed to a large silver door on the rear wall. "That leads to the walk-in cooler. We all kind of jump in, as time allows, and serve as sous chef. Cut up the lettuce for hamburgers, fill the salad dressing containers, et cetera. Our main rush starts about seven, and the noon crowd starts building by eleven." He turned to her. "Guess this might be a good time to ask if you've ever done this kind of work before."

Allie nodded enthusiastically. "Oh, yes. I was a waitress in high school."

Her temporary boss looked relieved. "Good. You'll fit right in."

As promised, tourists started pouring into the tiny establishment as soon as the sun cleared the horizon. By nine, they were lining the sidewalk, a dozen or so deep.

While Allie hadn't waited tables for several years, it all came back to her quickly. She balanced heavy platters loaded with eggs and pancakes on her forearm like a pro, while carrying a carafe of hot coffee with her other hand. She smiled and took orders, waiting patiently as customers scanned the plastic menus and changed their minds multiple times. She bussed tables, wiped down counters, made more coffee each time the Bunn got low.

The Pig 'n' Pancake wasn't the only breakfast restaurant in town, but you wouldn't know it from the steady stream of customers. By mid-morning, she felt like she'd put in two days' worth of work.

She had just raised the hinged flip-lid and poured water into the top of the coffee brewer when she noticed a dark-haired guy slide into a seat at the counter. He wore gray dress slacks, a belt, and a blue button-down shirt that matched the color of his stormy-blue eyes—eyes that locked on her like magnets.

"Hey, there," he said. "I don't think I've seen you around."

"Just moved here." She grabbed the carafe, held it up. "Coffee?"

He nodded, slid the empty coffee cup on the counter toward her. "Sure."

She filled his mug and turned to grab a menu.

"You got a name?" he asked, still eyeing her.

"That depends on who's asking." She'd encountered his type—guys who were harmless but came on a little too strong.

"Then let me properly introduce myself. My name is Craig

Anthony." There was laughter in his voice, and something else. A slight arrogance that irritated her.

Trying to be polite, she conjured a smile. "You live here?"

"All my life."

"You like it?" she asked while returning the coffee pot to the hot plate on the counter behind her.

His eyes crinkled with amusement, like her question had somehow entertained him. "Must've, or I wouldn't have stayed." He studied her so long that it became unnerving.

The door opened then, causing the bell above to tinkle.

In walked Cameron Davis. He sauntered over, slid into the barstool next to Craig. The two men nodded, assessing each other the way men sometimes do.

Cam smiled, though Allie was beginning to realize that there was a difference—small, but perceptible. Sometimes that smile was genuine, and sometimes it was just for show, a curtain hiding his real thoughts.

Craig Anthony stood, tossed a bill on the counter. "Keep the change," he said, gathering his jacket.

"Aren't you going to finish your coffee?" she asked, confused.

"Naw. I'm late for a meeting." He tipped his head. "Nice to have met you."

"Likewise," she said, more to be polite than anything.

When the door closed behind him, Cam reached for the menu the other guy left untouched on the counter. "I see you met Craig Anthony."

She busied herself by wiping the counter with a wet rag. "Well, yes. I mean, he introduced himself," she clarified. "You know him?"

"Craig Anthony is the mayor's son. And he's your competition," he warned.

Allie frowned. "Competition?"

Cam opened the menu, scanned the inside. "He owns Anthony Charters. Last year, he built a brand spanking new marina across the bay from where you live and now owns a fleet of over twenty boats. Might say he's gobbled up more than one independent fishing company in recent years. Seems to have endless funding, thanks to his mother. Craig has earned a reputation. Around here, he's known as the Codfather."

"The Codfather?" She suppressed a giggle.

Cameron closed his menu and placed it on the counter. "I'll have a ham and cheese omelet."

Allie tucked away the knowledge, and the fact Cam didn't seem to care for that Anthony guy. She scribbled the order on her tiny tablet, ripped out the page, and stuck it on the order wheel. "Order up," she called out.

Despite the crowd waiting for their orders to be taken, she couldn't help but ask, "You don't seem to like that Anthony guy much."

"I like him just fine," Cameron told her. "I just don't trust the guy."

She nodded, knowing there was likely more to the warning he wasn't saying, a thought she carried with her when she headed back to the kitchen to fill some syrup bottles.

When Cam's order was up, she slid his plate in front of him. "So, you looked like you were having fun last night. What else can people do around here for entertainment?"

"Well, Pacific Bay isn't known for being a social hub. The locals often make their own fun. I think Ryan might really enjoy crabbing. I'd be happy to take him sometime," he offered. "And you, if you're interested."

"Sure, we'd like that." A man at a table by the front door waved her over. "Well, the customers call." She pointed.

He grinned. "Yes, they sure do. By the way, have you found a captain yet?"

She shook her head as she grabbed some menus.

"Well, let me ask around—see what I can do."

"Thanks," she told him. "I really appreciate the help. With everything."

The steady current of breakfast customers barely slowed before the lunch crowd showed up. By two o'clock, her feet were killing her. Her back ached and she couldn't remember taking a restroom break, let alone eating anything.

Muncy noticed as well. He took her by the arm and pulled her aside. "Why don't you get on out of here? Won't get busy until dinnertime, and we've got that covered."

Allie gave him a look brimming with appreciation. "Thanks, Muncy. I'll see you tomorrow?"

"Yeah, see you tomorrow."

She pulled off her apron and hung it, then glanced at her watch as she hurried out the door. If she picked up the pace, she might still have time to make it to City Hall.

The air was warm outside, with a slight breeze coming in off the shoreline, bringing with it the smells of the ocean. A scattering of seagulls flew overhead, gliding on invisible airstreams. Occasionally, one would dip and scoop up something off the sidewalk ahead of her.

It was a short walk to City Hall, which ended up being a nondescript storefront with "City of Pacific Bay" painted on the large window facing the street. Allie stopped at the door, adjusted the hem of her shirt and pushed the door open.

Several clerks sat behind mismatched desks, their attention buried in the computer screens before them. One held a phone to her ear. "Yes, I understand what you're saying. City Council meets the first Tuesday of every month, and all meetings are open to the public. I urge you to attend and bring up your concerns then."

There was a counter against the back wall with windows.

Despite the fact no one was waiting at the windows, a gal at a desk nearest the front door looked up and told her to take a number.

"Thanks," Allie told her and pulled a ticket—number 663. The neon sign on the wall said, "Now serving 441."

Before Allie could point out the situation, the clerk stopped her by holding up an open palm. "Just wait until you're called," she said.

Allie shrugged and took a seat on a stiff wooden bench to the right of the front door. She held tight to her bag on her lap and fashioned in her mind how quickly the process might go. Surely, this wouldn't take long, given how no one was in line ahead of her.

She was wrong.

Nearly twenty minutes later, she was finally called to an open window. The clerk was a young girl who looked to be barely out of high school. She had blonde hair drawn back into a ponytail with a ribbon.

Allie stared. Were those unicorns?

"Well, hey. The City of Pacific Bay is here to serve. How can we help you?" she recited in a sing-song voice.

Allie pushed her paperwork through the open window. "I need a boat license, please."

The clerk's expression sobered. "Oh, I see."

"Is there a problem?" Allie asked, tamping down her annoyance.

"Wait here." The girl scooped up the documents and disappeared behind a wooden door.

A few minutes later, a woman appeared, following the girl from the counter. She wore a red short-sleeved dress tailored to her silhouette and a strand of pearls at her neckline—a definite statement piece. And, they looked *real*.

Allie thought the lady could have been a sister to that lady who often appeared on national television, the head of some political party. She wasn't, of course, but looked about that age, wore her dark-brown hair in the same style, and pursed her lips in the same manner.

Her coordinating red heels made a clacking noise against the shiny tiled floor as she stepped up to the window. "Hello, I'm Mayor Barbara Anthony," she said, introducing herself. "Could you come on back?" The stylish woman pointed to an access door at the end of the counter.

"Uh, sure." Allie frowned slightly and moved for the door. "Is there a problem?"

She could see where her son got his looks.

"I'm afraid Tarver allowed the liability insurance to expire. The city of Pacific Bay can't issue you a license without proper coverage." The mayor took a seat behind her desk. She motioned for Allie to sit as well. "I'm sure you understand how, especially in this situation where you intend to take tourists out—"

"Oh, yes. I understand." Allie sank into the offered chair. Her cheeks warmed. "And, that was certainly on my list." As if to prove the point, Allie dug in her purse and pulled out a little spiral-bound tablet.

Mayor Anthony straightened in her chair. "There's a second issue—that of no licensed captain."

Allie wanted to explain her intentions regarding that matter as well. Even so, her gut told her this woman might be more foe than friend. She simply nodded, her hands folded in her lap.

Mayor Anthony opened her desk drawer, withdrew a piece of paper, and slid it across the polished wooden desktop. "Here's the name of someone who is available. I urge you to give him a call."

Allie ignored the squeeze in her chest, smiled and took the paper. Without looking at it, she slipped it in her bag. "Thank you. I would be happy to include him in the candidates I'll be talking with."

"Excellent. I think you'll find Oswald Sanders a cut above most when it comes to this industry. I'm sure you'll find him more than suitable." Mayor Anthony drilled her with a look. "I know his background, which could expedite the process here in the office. Otherwise, background checks—well, sometimes those take weeks, even months."

Allie's mind raced. No way was she going to hire someone based on this woman's recommendation. She responded with a carefully controlled tone. "I—I'll be in touch with him."

Out in the parking lot, she slammed the key into the slot and yanked the car door open.

She could almost hear her mama telling her not to assign sinister motives to the mayor's actions too quickly. Only the good Lord knew what was inside someone's heart. But if her sweet mama were here, walking right next to her—Allie would point out that at least one critter in the Lord's perfect garden had turned out to be nothing but a snake.

ALLIE SAT at the tiny round table across from Ryan, scouring the cards in her hand. She shuffled the eight in front of the seven, stared. Seconds later, she moved the card back to where it'd been.

"C'mon, Mom."

She changed her mind, moved her cards again. "So, what did you do all day while I was gone?"

"Nothing," he told her. "It was so boring."

"You didn't go near the water, did you?"

He shook his head. "No, of course not. I did everything you told me to."

"Good." She studied her cards.

"Mom. C'mon, it's your turn, and I've been waiting at least twenty minutes now."

She looked up. "You so exaggerate." A satisfied grin sprouted on her face as she placed her cards down on the table. "Gin!"

Dejected, Ryan let his own cards fall to the table. He folded his arms on top of the cards and dropped his head to the table.

Allie gave her son a pat on the arm. "Oh, honey." She glanced at the clock on the wall, feeling like a heel. "It's only ten. Do you want to play Monopoly? You can be the banker."

He shook his head. "Nah, I'm kind of gamed out, Mom."

"You want to watch some television? I know we don't have cable, but *Star Wars* is on the Movie Network tonight. It's one of your favorites. I could pop some popcorn— No wait, we're out of popcorn." She looked over at him, hopeful. "We could spread some peanut butter on soda crackers?"

"I think I'll just go to bed." His shoulders sagged as he moved to kiss her good night.

Her heart squeezed into a tight knot. "Ryan?"

"Yeah, Mom?"

"I'm working to make things different, you know? I mean, I admit things are really tight right now. Every penny has to go to getting that boat up and running so it can bring us some cash flow."

Her son nodded. "Yeah, it's okay. I know, Mom." He trudged toward his room.

"Don't forget to brush your teeth," she called out after him. "And put your dirty clothes in the hamper."

Allie cleaned up the cards then wandered outside onto the deck. A foghorn sounded from across the bay where lights lining the shoreline twinkled brilliantly.

In Texas, the air smelled flat—and hot. Here in Pacific Bay, the breeze carried a hint of the fog rolling in, and with it, the smell of the ocean.

Allie breathed in deeply, let the salty air clear her head.

Ryan was homesick, she could tell. He hadn't made any friends yet. He'd been by her side working himself half to death. It was pretty hard to meet a good buddy when he never had time to go be a kid.

That had to change.

She'd seen the way he'd looked longingly at the families down on the beach. At the dads showing their kids how to fly kites and build sandcastles.

Deacon Ray Barrett was not the best human being on the face of the earth—but no doubt Ryan missed his dad.

Allie wandered back inside, picked up her cell phone off the coffee table and opened the contacts, scrolling until she saw Deacon Ray's name appear. She bit at her lip.

Maybe she could convince Deacon Ray to call Ryan, make it appear like it was his idea. That might be enough to brighten her boy a bit. She pushed her personal concerns aside, pressed send.

Immediately, a message appeared on the face of her phone. The number was no longer in service.

Allie sighed, slipped the phone into her jean's pocket. Deacon Ray had likely left his phone bill unpaid and had his service cut off—again.

Her head tilted toward the dark sky overhead, filled with a yearning she didn't quite understand. This new start was shadowed with far more pitfalls than she'd expected. Perhaps the only way to get rid of the shadows was to turn off the lights, to stop running from the darkness and face what she feared, head-on.

She was determined. Somehow, she was going to find a way to put a smile back on Ryan's face. She'd start by easing way up on chores, find more ways for him to have a good time.

Despite the setbacks, she'd work to get that boat registered and ready for business. She'd find a captain, hopefully one of her own choosing. And there would eventually be more employees. She'd been noodling ideas over, and maybe she could apply for a loan. That way she could afford the insurance she'd need. With *Reel Time* up and running, she could pay the loan funds back in no time.

For the first time that day, she dared a tiny smile.

Sometimes all a person needed was a good plan.

8

"I'm sorry, Miss Barrett. You're just not a good risk." The man sitting across the desk from Allie gave her a sympathetic look. "There's no collateral to secure the loan, no unencumbered assets. You're making payments on a car with little to no existing value."

Allie huffed in exasperation. "You're wrong, sir. I do have assets." She pointed to the document in his hand. "I listed everything on the loan application. I have a boat. *Reel Time* is docked and waiting for me to load her up with people who want to go fishing."

"I'm afraid the boat is nearly fifty years old and is still technically in your uncle's name. Besides that, you aren't registered with the city, and you have no insurance."

"But that's why I need the loan. To cover the insurance so that I can register the boat. And I need to hire a captain." Earlier that morning, she'd had another gut punch. A liability insurance binder would cost tens of thousands of dollars. Who knew the amount would be so significant?

The funds in her savings would never stretch far enough to

bridge her living expenses and cover her business start-up costs. She needed this loan.

"Please, if you'd just give me a chance. I promise you, I'm a hard worker. And I'm honest. I'll pay back every cent. No matter what."

His dimpled hand rubbed the top of his balding head. "I'm sorry. Securing a business loan simply doesn't work that way."

The loan officer glanced at his wristwatch. "Is there anyone who might co-sign? A father? Brother? A rich old aunt?"

Allie groaned inside. If she had a rich old aunt, would she be here begging for financial help? She rubbed her aching forehead. "No. Just me."

"A bigger down payment?" He suggested. "Another income stream besides the temporary waitressing job?"

She lifted her head. "No, I guess I don't." She collected her purse and stood.

It was then she saw a familiar face walking toward them. She groaned a second time.

Mayor Anthony smiled broadly. "Well, hello again." She reached her hand to shake Allie's. "Good to see you, Ms. Barrett."

She smiled weakly. "Yes, good to see you too." Okay, that was a lie. But what else was she supposed to say?

"I'm sorry we couldn't make you the loan. I hope Charlie was able to help you understand why."

Allie frowned. "I'm not sure I—"

"I'm president of the board," Mayor Anthony explained.

"And the bank's majority stockholder and head of the loan committee," Charlie added.

Dread crept up Allie's back, as cold as a dead man's fingers. "I—I didn't know that."

Mayor Anthony's face broke into a wry smile. "If it helps, I will authorize a small unsecured personal loan to help you out until you can land on your feet—say five hundred dollars?"

Allie's spirit sunk. She shook her head. "Uh, no, thank you. That's—well, it's not enough."

Mayor Anthony shook her head in feigned sympathy. "I hope you understand we'd make the loan, but there are rules in place."

"Rules, of course. I understand." She was learning this town had more rules than a game of Monopoly, and she'd just pulled the *Go to Jail* card. All she wanted was to slink out the door while she still had some dignity in place.

Mayor Anthony touched her arm. "I do have an idea. I'm not sure if you're aware, but my son owns a charter boat company—a much larger enterprise than what you're contemplating. If I speak with him, he might be willing to buy you out. He'd be doing you a favor, really. Running a charter fishing business is difficult, even more if you are a woman and you're unfamiliar with the industry."

Allie frowned. "Buy me out?"

"I don't think you really have any other options, do you?"

The full impact of what was going down hit Allie. This woman had Boardwalk and Park Place and wanted all the railroads too. And as banker, she wasn't about to dole out any currency to her opponent.

She recalled Cameron's warning—the one she'd brushed off, not understanding the potential of what he was telling her.

So, this was what she was up against.

She felt like a cartoon strip—the one where the football kept getting pulled out from under Charlie Brown's feet and he landed on his back with everyone laughing.

She couldn't help it. Tears stung at the back of her eyes as she stared back at Mayor Anthony, trying to keep her lip from visibly quivering.

"I—I don't think so." It was all she could think to say.

She grabbed her purse and blindly headed for the door. At

the curb, she paused and looked both ways, wiped her tears with the back of her hand.

She wanted to believe life was fair, but sometimes you couldn't argue things would always turn around for good—even for those who tried to live right. Plans didn't always turn out. Dreams and hope could get dashed by people and situations outside your control.

No matter how carefully she'd constructed this new start in life, she'd let Ryan down—herself down.

She needed time to think—to sort out this mess.

Blinded by tears, Allie stepped off the curb and headed for her Blazer, which was parked directly across the street.

"Look out!"

Before Allie could discover who yelled the warning, she heard a loud screech, followed by an impact she never saw coming.

9

Allie pulled the hospital bed covers up to her chin, barely able to hold back another wave of tears. She blinked hard and glanced around the room.

The room was bright and impersonal, with a window overlooking the parking lot. Beside her bed's silver metal rails stood a table heaped with crumpled tissues.

She knew she should be thankful the accident hadn't been worse. If that kid on his bicycle hadn't hit his brakes like he did, she'd have surely been a goner. Instead, she'd suffered a bruised hip, a strained shoulder, and a severely wilted ego. Let alone the dent in her checkbook.

The ride in the ambulance alone would cost thousands.

The notion of mounting medical expenses on top of all the business expenses looming—well, it was more than she could handle.

At the thought, fresh tears sprung and flowed freely down her smudged cheeks. Not bothering to hold in her emotional collapse, she wailed out loud. Who cared if someone heard her sobs?

Allie winced as the IV in her arm pulled and pinched in the

process. Why keep looking at the bright side when reality always seemed to tarnish her best intentions?

The door opened and a nurse marched in. "Well, honey. The doctor cleared you to go home."

Allie looked up, hopeful. She dried her tears. "You mean it? Good." She threw the covers back, then remembered her modesty and pulled them back up. "Uh, could you—"

Two hours later, she was dressed and ready to go. Before leaving, the nurse helped her into an arm sling. "You'll want to wear this for at least a week. Keep that elbow stable until it heals."

Allie stuck her lip out in a pout. Her head hurt. Her hip ached. "There goes my job at the Pig 'n' Pancake," she muttered out loud. "A one-handed waitress isn't much good to anybody."

The nurse gave her a sympathetic smile and helped her into the mandatory wheelchair for her ride to the lobby. They wheeled down the hallway, past the nurses' station and a wall of beeping and hissing monitors when Allie noticed a familiar figure walking toward them holding a bouquet of flowers in his hand.

"Hey, where you going?" Cameron Davis asked, concern written all over his face. "I was on my way to see you."

She gave an exaggerated shrug. "Nice bed, great mattress. And the room had a beautiful view of the bay. Sadly, I couldn't afford the room rate. Not on my salary." She fought the urge to cry again.

He moved to her side, looked up at the nurse. "I got it from here."

"Hey, Cam. We're having a bit of a difficult time," she said, talking as though Allie were a child. She then nodded and handed over the wheelchair handles into his capable hands. "Her things are in this bag." She pointed to the plastic sack hanging from one of the handles.

Cam noticed her tear-stained face. He grabbed a tissue

from a box on a nearby table and handed it to her. "Here, blow your nose."

She pulled back. "No. I'm good." Instead, she used the back of her good arm.

"Oh, don't cry. Things are already looking up. I talked to the guys down at the Search and Rescue office, and several were willing to moonlight, switch shifts in order to help you out—gratis."

She looked at him through tear-rimmed lashes. "What are you saying?"

"The guys, well—they are all certified boat captains. They'll take turns pitching in, knowing you're in a pinch. Help you until you get your sea legs underneath you, so to speak. When a little income starts rolling in, you can hire yourself a full-time captain." He paused, looked at her meaningfully. "Me and Dad have been talking you up at the Pig 'n' Pancake. Lots of tourists come in asking for recommendations. We can send a lot of business your way."

That really put her over the top. She covered her face with her hands and cried even louder.

"Ah, c'mon. Don't cry," he said.

"It'll be over in a minute," she told him in a muffled voice.

She could hear a scraping sound as the front doors automatically opened and he wheeled her out into the sunshine.

A little embarrassed about letting her emotions get away from her, Allie let her hands slowly drop. "Guess I'm just feeling a little sorry for myself."

Cameron studied her for a moment. "I'll listen if you want to talk."

She lowered her gaze, picked at the wadded tissue in her hand. "Well, I've been sitting here thinking how I was raised to believe I could do anything I set my mind to, but I think I've bitten off far more than I can chew this time." She sniffled. "I mean, I've been raising this kid all by myself, making all these mistakes. I thought I was doing the right thing bringing him to Oregon. Lately, I've been wondering if everything I've done over the past six months has been a serious miscalculation. I'm likely damaging my son for life." A fresh trickle of tears streamed down her cheek. "Add to that the fact I have a concussion, a bruised hip, and a sprained shoulder that hurts like the dickens—and well, life just sucks right now."

Cam nodded sympathetically. "Life can throw some curveballs, but you're handling things the best you can. Doubt anyone could do it better, given the circumstances."

"That's not even the worst part," she told him.

His eyebrows lifted. "No?"

"I'm thirty-three years old, and all I do at night is play cards with my kid or watch television!" She leaned back and sniffed, an ugly nasal-plugged kind of sniff.

Suddenly, there was a commotion that drew her attention.

It'd been years since Allie had seen a man's bare backside. But suddenly, there in front of the nurses' station, a white-haired man, stooped with age, shuffled down the narrow hallway dressed in shirt, socks, and shoes, but no pants.

"Lester, did you forget something?" A buxom, middle-aged nurse with a blazing-red mass of curls scurried after the man. She stepped in front of him, hands planted on her hips. "You go straight back to your room and put your britches on."

"I don't remember where I put 'em." Lester glanced in Allie's direction, a smile teasing at the corners of his mouth.

The nurse snatched the walkie-talkie belted at her side and pressed her thumb against the button. "Mona, I need some help in the lobby. It's Lester again."

In no time, a younger woman in nursing scrubs joined them.

"Mona, let's get Lester back to his room and find him some pants." The redhead then smiled apologetically in their direction. "Sorry about the show, folks." She turned and followed Mona and Lester down the hall.

Cam laughed as they made their way into the lobby. "Well, there's something you don't see every day." He paused, waited for the automatic glass doors to open.

"No, I don't suppose so." Allie waited for Cam to lock the wheels of the chair in place before she lifted and took a few unsteady steps.

"Hey, easy now," Cam said, putting his arm around her shoulder to keep her from falling. His pickup was parked under the portico.

Cam scurried to the passenger door, opened it, and held out his hand. "We'll just take it slow. Nice and easy." He put his arm around her waist, helped her in. "You good?"

She nodded.

He shut the door, then moved for the driver's side and climbed in beside her.

"You didn't have to do this," she told him. "I mean, I could've called Uber."

He shook his head. "Nonsense. This is what friends do for one another."

She studied Cam's face. His presence brought her unexpected peace. "Thanks. I—I need a friend," she admitted. "Especially since my life is such a mess."

"Let's take a good, hard look at reality," he said, starting the engine. "You might not think so, but you're doing a great job raising your son. Ryan's polite, says please and thank you. Respects his elders. Appears you haven't damaged him all that much. And your concussion is mild. Your hip is bruised, but it'll heal. So will that shoulder. You'll just have to manage the pain for a day or so. I asked the doctor."

Allie flipped her head in his direction, shocked. "What about HIPAA?"

His eyebrows raised. "HIPAA?"

"The privacy laws."

Cam chuckled. "This is Pacific Bay. And the doctor is my golf partner." As if that answer was wholly sufficient, he pulled his car out of the parking lot and onto the street leading to Main.

She nodded.

"And about that sagging social life?" He stopped at the light, flipped on his blinker. "That's easily fixed. Next time you're asked—say yes." He wore a self-satisfied smirk that should have been unattractive. Yet, his grin was somehow endearing.

She smiled, but it was hesitant. "What about you?"

He laughed. "You asking me about my social life?"

"Yes, I am."

The light turned green. He said nothing for several seconds, then coughed as if to clear his throat. "There's a lady in Portland who cooks me dinner on occasion." He paused, pressed down on the gas. "Nothing serious, really. And, it's a fair drive, but—" He shrugged and smiled. "Well, I have a social life."

Allie turned in the seat and looked at him. "Hmm. Well, I'm happy for you."

His blue eyes twinkled with amusement. "Oh, are you now?"

He eased his pickup into an empty spot behind where her car was parked. "Okay, here we are." He glanced across the passenger seat. "You feeling better?"

"Yes," she admitted.

That brought a smile to his face. "Well, I think you're going to make it. Your color's good. Your business prospects are looking up. And whale season is still coming at the end of the year, regardless." He smiled, shut off the engine. "You only have one problem."

She looked up. "What's that?"

"That shirt you're wearing." He pointed, grinning. "I think it's buttoned wrong."

She glanced down. In horror, she discovered in a hurry to get dressed, she'd skipped a button when fastening her blouse. The result was a gaping opening at her chest.

"Well, thanks a lot." She fist-punched him using her good arm. "Why didn't you say something? I mean, you stood by and let me walk in public like that. Why don't you just parade me up and down the streets of Pacific Bay while you're at it?"

He tossed his head back, laughing. "Embrace it. Might help your social life."

ALLIE LEANED back in the newly painted Adirondack chair and watched Ryan dip his rag into the bucket. He climbed back up on the stepladder and continued wiping the dirty glass window.

"Ryan, watch what you're doing. You're missing the entire side over here." She pointed.

He sighed. "How many more of these do I have to do?"

"All of them," she reported, frustrated she couldn't climb up and do the chore herself. She'd made a promise to lighten his chores, but what choice did she have? The job needed done, and she was in no position physically to do it without him. Despite her sprained shoulder, she stood and grabbed the hose coiled on the deck. "Here, use this."

Ryan climbed down, took the hose, and heaved it back up the stepladder. He pointed it at the window. Allie hobbled over and turned on the spigot.

Several minutes later, Ryan looked down at her. "Is this good enough?"

She noted a couple of streaks. Given the look on her son's face, she didn't press the matter and waved him down. "Yeah, honey. It's fine."

He tossed the hose down while she turned off the water.

The postal truck drove up, stopped. The mailman got out and walked the mail to her. "Sorry to hear about your little accident."

She smiled and took the stack of envelopes from him. "Thanks, Joe," she said, rifling through the flyers and white envelopes. Three were from medical providers.

She sliced one open, nearly choked when she saw the amount due. As much as she'd like to shield her son from the harsh reality, she knew better than to paint this weed a rose.

She put her free hand on her hip. "Ryan, we have a problem. We're counting every penny here. You've got to help me out. You can't just leave the lights on all over the place. And you can't spend any more money on gaming apps." She held up her phone. "In fact, we may have to downgrade our cell plan."

Ryan bent and wrapped up the hose and placed it neatly on the hook by the spigot. "But, Mom. I watch You Tube on your phone."

Allie took the wet rag, wiped down the front door, taking care not to jiggle her injured shoulder. "I'm sorry, but we've fallen on some hard times. I mean, harder than normal. Understand?"

He said nothing. Instead, he walked over and dumped his bucket of water.

She watched him. "Because we're on our own."

He slowly nodded. The worry sprouting on his face stopped her short. Perhaps she'd leaned toward too much reality.

She walked over, pulled him into a tight hug. "Look, my mama used to say things have a way of working out. We're going to get through this. We'll end up just fine. You'll see."

"Yeah." He nodded.

She stepped back, took him by the shoulders, and looked him in the eyes. "We'll be all right—right?"

He nodded—a bit more enthusiastically this time.

She gave him a playful shake. "Right?"

Finally, he broke into a full grin. "Right!"

Okay," she said. "Let's get all this put away and start in the attic. There's a bunch of stuff up there, and we may be able to sell some of it."

She had a digger of a time shimmying up the ladder, knowing full well her doctor would have a cow if he saw her betraying his orders to keep that shoulder still. She'd have to remind him, of course, that she might not have to take such a risk if he was willing to write off his bill.

"Be careful, Mom."

"I am," she assured her son as she ignored the pain and quickly moved to take the weight off her bad hip.

The attic was dark and musty. Boxes were stacked haphazardly, and there was no shortage of thick cobwebs—the kind that clung to your hair and clothes.

"Gosh, Mom. It's yucky up here." He gave her a look that said he'd rather be anywhere else.

Allie donned her brightest smile. "Let's just think of it as a treasure hunt. We're pirates, and—"

Ryan rolled his eyes. "Mom, I'm eleven."

"Too old for those games, huh?" The notion made her sad. The same kind of sad she'd felt the first time she noticed the dimples were gone from his hands. The emotion she'd felt when his first tooth fell out, leaving him with a goofy grin. They were supposed to grow up, but the process could be a lot like watching your heart walk out the door.

"Here, Mom. You sit down," he instructed. "I'll carry the boxes over to you."

She awarded him with a smile and nested herself into a comfortable position on the floor. "Sounds like a plan."

The first box was filled with odd pieces of faded Tupperware and misfit lids. Another held worn towels, many with the hems unraveled. There were also several clear plastic bread sacks filled with hotel soaps and those tiny bottles of shampoo.

Uncle Tarver was a bit of a hoarder.

Allie smiled, wishing she'd had the opportunity to meet her mother's brother. Many times, she'd suspected his letters to Mama contained money. She'd like to thank him for that.

Ryan handed her another box. "This stuff is nothing but junk."

She tended to agree. The last box held an array of eclectic items: a tiny silver spoon, an aqua blue tie with what looked to be a coffee stain. She pulled out a pair of binoculars in a battered leather case. The strap had turned stiff.

"Hey, Ryan?"

"Yeah," he said, digging his way to another stack of boxes.

"Come put these in a pile over there. These old binoculars might bring some money down at the pawnshop."

She continued digging through the box, hoping to find items of value. Instead, she yanked out a frayed fishing vest, the pockets full of bird feathers. She sighed. "Take this too. But first, dump the pockets."

Without looking up, Ryan muttered, "Hey, Mom?"

"Yeah?"

"I think this uncle guy must've liked pickles. This box is filled with pickle jars."

Allie scowled. "Pickle jars?" She motioned. "Bring them over, let me see."

Ryan picked up the box and carried it over, set it in front of her. "The jars have something in them."

Allie pulled one out of the box. Curious, she unscrewed the lid and pulled out one of many tiny white envelopes. The effort proved difficult, given how tightly they were packed inside the jar.

"What do you think this is?" She flipped the envelope over and examined it.

Ryan got on his knees, leaned over to take a look. "Open it," he said.

Allie fingers worked under the seal and tore open the envelope. Her eyes flew open wide, and she gasped. "Oh, my goodness!"

Ryan leaned closer for a better look. "What is it?"

Allie unfurled a tightly curled one-hundred-dollar bill. And another.

She stared at her son. "Ryan, it's money." She extracted another bill—another, then another. "There are lots of them." She put the jar aside, dug back in the box. "Help me."

They both extracted another jar only to find the same thing. A third jar, the same.

Allie's hand went to her chest. "Ryan! There are hundreds of these bills. Hundreds!"

Ryan yanked off the lid of another box. "This one has pickle jars!" He pulled off the lids of several more boxes. "So do these!"

Allie grabbed several of the bills in her fists and flung them in the air, letting the money rain down over her head. "Ryan," she said. "I'm growing very fond of pickles."

10

Allie loved that time of the morning before the sun came up, when only a hint of light bordered the horizon. Particularly on this special morning when everything she'd hoped for was miraculously falling into place.

After all the past months and financial obstacles, the day for *Reel Time's* maiden voyage had finally arrived—well, at least the first voyage under her management. The very thought was thrilling, the kind of exhilaration that created a buzzy feeling in her stomach.

She stood on the dock, taking it all in—passengers lined up waiting to load wearing sweatshirt hoodies with thermos containers in hand, the way they quietly spoke of sea bass limits. A couple of men discussed how many knots the diesel Cummins engine would push.

She loved the mist-filled air that carried the aroma of the briny bait being loaded into the wells and the way the water lapped against the shiny exterior of the boat—the freshly painted name on the side.

It had only taken a few weeks to get the insurance and licensing in place after finding Uncle Tarver's pickle jars. The look on Mayor Anthony's face had been priceless when she'd strutted out of her office door to find Allie standing at the counter, getting the paperwork properly notarized.

"Ms. Barrett, what a surprise!" Her expression clearly indicated how shocked she was to see her back. "What are we helping you with today?" she asked, coming over and peeking over the clerk's shoulder.

The clerk's ponytail swung as she turned to the mayor. "Good news! Allie's documentation is all in order. We're issuing the license."

Mayor Anthony's face darkened. "Oh?" She grabbed the stack of papers. Her red-polished nails gleamed as her fingers rifled through them. "The insurance is in place?"

Allie smiled confidently. "Yes. It's all there and in order."

Mayor Anthony visibly drew back. The pencil-thin line of her lips signaled she'd rather die of shark bite than issue that license. She forced a smile. "Good. Well, I hope Candy is taking excellent care of you."

"Oh, yes. She is." Allie had to try desperately not to grin. "Thank you."

Even now, a fresh pang of satisfaction filled her as she lifted the Styrofoam cup of hot coffee to her lips, took a careful sip.

Captain Paul signaled. "We're ready."

She nodded, a fresh thrill moving through her. She put her hand on Ryan's shoulder "C'mon, buddy. Let's board."

Cameron Davis had been true to his promise and had helped her secure the services of a highly qualified licensed captain. She'd soon added him to her payroll.

Paul Hardy was a recent retiree of the Coast Guard after over thirty years of service. He'd grown up in Pacific Bay. His wife, Darlene, was president of the Chamber of Commerce and had delivered a large basket filled with Tillamook cheese and wine to welcome her to the business community.

Today's run would primarily be a bottom-fishing trip.

They'd drop crab pots on the way out and pick them up on the return trip. They had eight guests—four men, two women and two teenagers, an extended family from New Mexico. According to Captain Paul, the manifest revealed these landlubbers had never been deep sea fishing before.

An apropos situation, as she'd had never served as skipper either, at least not officially. Allie took a deep breath and climbed on board. Like her Mama always said, there was a first time for everything.

Ryan helped her check the temperature on the bait well as Captain Paul went over the safety rules. "If any of you goes overboard, Allie will throw this life ring to you." He pointed to the bright-orange safety ring hanging on the side of the door leading into the cabin. "But don't panic. She'll also toss you a pole all baited with shrimp fry so you can fish until we pick you back up on the way back in to dock."

Everyone standing on deck laughed.

Captain Paul explained they'd be fishing for rockfish, lingcod, and cabezon. "Last week, the catch reports were heavy with snapper as well, and an occasional black bass. Regardless, the crew assures you'll all disembark with your baskets full of fish." That made everyone smile. "When you feel your line tug, yell 'Fish on!' That will signal to those around you to reel in their lines to prevent tangles."

Allie gave a few last-minute instructions to her son. "Remember, I'm going to be really busy. I won't be able to watch you. So, keep that life jacket on at all times. And make sure you stay back and don't get in the way when people are trying to fish."

"I will," he promised. "But, Mom?"

"Yeah?"

"Can I fish too?"

She tweaked his chin. "Of course, baby." She pointed to a

rod in the rack. "That one is your personal fishing pole. Only to be used by you."

"And can I help you take the fish off the lines?"

She chuckled. "If you want. You can also help me knot the buoys on the crab lines."

The trip ended up highly successful. The boat reached its limit, and they returned to dock by noon.

The family from New Mexico disembarked wearing wide grins. "Thank you! That was a lovely trip," one of the women told her as she unzipped her sweatshirt on her way to the filet tables. "We're going to ship our catch home. I'll think of this trip every time I serve those lovely fish."

Allie smiled, glad their first customers were delighted with the excursion. "I hope you'll join us again sometime."

The woman nodded. "Oh, yes. We plan to make this an annual event." She pushed a wad of bills into Allie's hand. "This is for you and your son. Thank you for everything."

Allie expressed her gratitude for the tip, unsure who had the better time—the guests or her.

She'd loved everything about the excursion. The frothy waves left in the wake of the boat as they cut through the gentle sea swells, the beauty of the distant shoreline, the line of hotels and condos barely visible against the backdrop of pines. Like the other passengers, she'd thrilled when they spotted a gray humpback spouting.

Warned about possible seasickness, she'd taken Dramamine the evening before to ward off any issues caused by the rise and fall of the vessel with the water swells. She'd also stayed well hydrated and remembered to focus on the horizon occasionally. Paul told her she'd eventually adjust, and she'd no longer be vulnerable to the malady.

Fortunately, those precautions had done their magic and she'd suffered no problems—despite the constant trips back and forth across the deck as people hooked fish.

Poor Ryan was not as lucky.

While she was hustling to keep lines baited and help reel in fish, Ryan made his way to the front of the boat. The bow bobbing up and down felt like a carnival ride to a kid who didn't know any better.

Within the first hour, he ended up with his head leaned over his arms on the table in the cabin, groaning that he felt nauseous. Poor baby spent the entire trip fighting the urge to throw up.

He still felt a little green under the gills when he stepped off the boat.

"Hey!" Cameron made his way up the dock to greet them. "How'd it all go this morning?"

Allie put her arm around Ryan's shoulders. "I'm afraid somebody's tummy didn't cooperate."

Cameron ruffled Ryan's hair. "Aw, that's too bad, buddy. Now that you're off the boat, you'll feel better really soon. But, hey, a little birdy tells me your birthday is tomorrow."

Ryan looked up at him, a smile starting to form. "Yeah, I'm going to be eleven."

Allie grinned. Her kid loved birthdays and had been waiting for this day. Upon learning they were moving to Oregon, he was so afraid they wouldn't celebrate. She's assured him his day would be special. She'd make sure of that.

Truth was, she'd been so distracted lately that she'd barely had time to focus on pulling together anything. Ryan hadn't made a lot of friends yet. She figured she'd hand him a hundred-dollar bill and let him buy anything he wanted. They'd never had the money to do something like that ever. Thanks to her uncle, she had the means now.

Cam grew thoughtful. "Look, I haven't passed this by your Mom yet, so hear me out when I say she'd have to give the okay first. But—" He looked at Allie. "I'd like to take both of you crabbing."

"Oh, wow! Can we, Mom?"

"Crabbing?" She did a quick mental review of the boat manifest, recalling they had no one booked for tomorrow. She'd checked earlier, knowing she wanted to have some time free to celebrate with Ryan. "Uh—sure. If you want to."

Ryan beamed. "I do. I saw a video on YouTube about it, and it looked really cool."

Cam rubbed his chin stubble. "On You Tube, huh?" He smiled. "Well, no video could possibly compete with the real thing." He pulled a tiny worn tide chart out of his back pocket, thumbed through it. "Best time is at slack right after high tide. Looks like that's about nine o'clock in the morning."

"Perfect," she said. "That will allow time for you to join us for his birthday breakfast."

"Yeah," Ryan said. "You don't want to miss birthday breakfast."

THE NEXT MORNING, Ryan woke to Allie sitting on the bottom of his bed holding a tiny wrapped box. "Well, it's about time Birthday Boy!" She thrust the box into his hands. "Open it."

Ryan's eyes widened. "What is it?"

"Open it. You'll see."

He tore the paper off, lifted the lid on the box. "A hundred dollars! For me?"

In her excitement, Allie clasped her hands together like it was her own birthday. "Yes, for you. I want you to buy anything you want—*anything!*"

Ryan lifted the bill out, examined it. "I've never held a hundred dollars of my very own."

She smiled. "It's going to be quite the birthday."

Breakfast was their standard celebration fare—an omelet filled with bacon *and* sausage with tons of melted cheese alongside a high stack of pancakes slathered in butter and syrup with a lit candle on top. Oh, and a can of Dr Pepper. Nutritional values all went out the window on your birthday.

"Thanks, Mom," Ryan said as she placed his plate on the table before him.

Cameron grinned from across the table. "That looks delicious!"

When they finished, they left the dirty dishes in the sink for later and made their way down to the marina and the dock located below the Pacific Bay Bridge. Cameron unloaded the equipment from the back of his pickup, and they carried it to an unoccupied spot at the end of the dock.

"Okay, the first thing we have to do is bait up," Cam explained.

He removed the lid of a white plastic bucket, reached in, and took out some mangled pieces of chicken.

"Oh man, that smells!" Ryan complained, holding his nose.

"Exactly. It's been rotting for days."

Allie quickly covered her nostrils with her hand. "I agree. It stinks!"

Cameron laughed and fastened the chicken to the bottom of a large round ring lined with netting and a draw line several yards long. "Watch and learn." He tossed the ring over the railing into the water below. The ring quickly sank out of sight.

Ryan ran and leaned over the railing. "Cool."

"Your turn," Cam said, pointing to another ring.

He didn't have to ask her son twice. Despite the foul aroma, Ryan ran over and grabbed some of the chicken meat and duplicated what he'd seen displayed. "Like this?" he said, checking to make sure he'd followed the steps properly.

Cam nodded. "You got it. Now toss the ring over the side."

Filled with excitement, Ryan did as he was told and flung the ring into the water. "Now what?"

Cam patted his shoulder. "Now, we wait." He turned to Allie. "I brought a ring for you too."

"I'll wait a bit," she told him with a timid smile.

The fact was, she enjoyed watching her son. It'd been a long time since she'd seen that level of happiness on his face.

It hadn't been easy on him, moving a half a country away, leaving all his friends and everything he'd known behind—including his father.

Sadly, Deacon Ray had made no attempt to call Ryan since they'd arrived in Oregon. And there had been no card in the mailbox for his birthday.

Allie let out a heavy sigh. Ryan deserved more than that.

Frankly, so did Deacon Ray. The fact he rarely thought of others and focused solely on his own self-interest was the byproduct of his own daddy. It was true what they say. The apple didn't fall far from the tree.

Still, she'd hoped Deacon Ray might be different with Ryan.

"Is it time yet?" Ryan asked, looking over the railing at the dark water below and barely able to contain his excitement.

Cameron checked his watch. "Yeah, I suppose."

"What do we do next?" Ryan took the gloves Cam handed him and pulled them on his hands.

"See this line?"

Ryan nodded, his face all serious. "Yup."

"Well, it's better if two of us work together. Here, take hold of this pull rope right here."

"Like this?"

"Yeah, that's good. Now I'm going to stand behind you and when I start counting, you start pulling. Got it?"

Ryan nodded. "Got it."

Cameron looked back at Allie, winked. "Okay, ready? Start pulling. One, two. One. two." Hand-over-hand, he pulled.

Ryan did the same.

Allie moved closer so she could get in on the action, but not too close. She didn't want to get in their way.

Soon, the ring broke the water's surface.

The boys kept pulling for all they were worth.

"Oh, my goodness! Look at that, Mom!"

The ring was filled with crabs—big spider-looking things with claws. She'd heard they were good to eat, but a girl didn't get a chance to eat a lot of crab in Texas. Especially someone on her budget.

"These are Dungeness crabs," Cam explained, placing the ring on the dock. As soon as he did, the mass of crabs went all directions. "Same as you pull in on the boat."

"They walk sideways, just like in the video," Ryan said, bending down for a better look.

"Don't touch," Cam warned. "Those claws can take a chunk of skin if you're not careful." He carefully lifted one of the larger crabs, turned it over. "See that?" He pointed to the underside. "If that apron there is wide like this one, it's a female. It's unlawful to keep females." He tossed the crab back into the water, grabbed another. "This one has a narrow apron. He's a male."

Ryan leaned over and nodded. "Yeah, I see."

Cameron took a measuring gauge out of his jacket pocket. "And you can't keep the males unless they are five and three-quarters inches long. About the size of a dollar bill measuring from shell tip to shell tip." He showed them how to measure. "See? This is a keeper." He tossed the crab into a waiting bucket and closed the lid.

Together, he and Ryan quickly went through their catch, tossing some back and securing the keepers in the bucket.

"Okay, get that ring baited back up and then we'll pull in the second ring." He looked over at her. "When we get done here, I'll help you cook and clean them, if you like."

"What do they taste like?" Ryan asked while he hooked a mangled chicken leg to the bottom of the ring.

"Like a little piece of heaven," Cam told him, his face playful, almost impish. "Especially when you dip the crabmeat in melted butter with lemon and a dab of fresh garlic."

He looked back at Allie, smiled. "I think the kid's a natural." He opened the top to his cooler, pulled out a cold Dr Pepper." He held up the can to her. "Heard you Texans like these."

She thanked him and took the can, cocked her head. "So, I heard something too."

"Yeah, what's that?"

"I heard the bank where I deposited Tarver's pickle jar money isn't the only establishment in town extending money to those in need."

He raised an eyebrow, grinned. "What do you mean?"

She popped the top of the can. "Word has it Jenny Zipp, down at the nursing home, was taken off Medicare because of a computer error, right when she needed a wheelchair for a broken back. Andy Perkins was fired two days before his pension started after thirty years working at the mill. And there's a kid down at the high school—the valedictorian—who didn't have the money he needed to front the plane tickets to fly for an interview at Harvard."

Cameron opened his can. "That so?"

"My friends in Texas would call you a dad-gum saint."

That made him laugh. "Well, you could tell those friends I'm definitely no saint."

There was a hesitation. "So, why are you being so nice to a single mother and her kid?"

He looked her in the eyes. "Oh, that one's easy."

"Yeah? How so?"

He stood, wiped his hands on a rag. "Thought I'd like to start socializing a little closer to home."

11

For several seconds, Allie stood silent.

Just what did he mean by that?

She averted her gaze, coughed, and pointed to the empty crab ring resting against the pier. "Is it my turn?"

He pocketed the rag, a grin sprouting on his face. "Yeah, sure. C'mon."

She followed him down the pier several yards, thinking about his visit to the hospital as they walked. In her highly emotional state, she'd not only inadvertently given him a peek inside her blouse, she'd given him a window into her empty spaces. She was lonely, and she let him see that. Now, he was teasing her.

Yet something told her his motive was not that simple—perhaps it was the look in the depth of his green eyes, the suggestion she saw as he continued to stare at her, how he watched her even now as he set the crab ring down.

When he finally averted his gaze, she swallowed, stole a curious glance at him. "Cam?"

"Yeah?"

"What did you mean—that comment?" She struggled to

keep her voice light, held her breath, and waited for him to clarify. Cam was simply making small talk. Surely he wasn't suggesting he'd like to have a relationship that extended beyond friendship.

He looked directly at her. "I meant, I'd like to take you out sometime." He paused, watched for her reaction. "As in a date."

"You do know cannabis is the devil's lettuce, right?"

That made him laugh. He made an imaginary mark in the air—his way of saying "score one for you."

Ryan waved at her from down the pier.

Allie returned the wave before parking her hands on her hips. Her heart pounded at a ridiculous rate. "Look, I'm—well, I know what I said in the hospital about feeling like a nun and all. But—"

He bent and fastened a piece of chicken to the bottom of the crab ring. "But, you're afraid."

"I'm not afraid."

He shrugged. "Okay, you're not afraid." He handed the ring to her. "Here, give this a toss."

She did as he instructed and heaved the crab ring over the side of the pier, watching as the blue circle faded from view as it sunk deep into the water.

She straightened the hem of her shirt, now wishing she'd worn something a bit nicer. Her pink T-shirt, maybe. She looked good in that color. And she should have worn her hair loose instead of tied back into a ponytail.

Oh, who was she kidding? She wasn't a teenager who needed to primp just because some guy handed her a clever line.

She'd fallen for lines before. Like the night she met Deacon Ray. He could knock a hole in the wind with his malarkey. Like his, "Do you have a map? Because I'm getting lost in those blue eyes of yours."

She'd stared back at him, told him her eyes were brown.

That lanky Texan with a pocket full of charm simply grinned. "Doesn't matter darlin', because this here is love at first sight."

After stumbling into that bucket of nonsense, how could she trust herself to know any better now?

Cam stepped to the edge of the pier, leaned his elbows on the rail, and stared out across the water. "Look, if I—"

Allie quickly reached and touched his elbow. "No. It's all right. I mean, I'm just letting all this sink in a minute."

He nodded slowly. "And?"

"And, maybe I'd like you to socialize closer to home as well, but I've got a kid to think about. I can't just—"

"I'm not asking for a five-course meal and then to stay for breakfast. We can take things slow. Get to know one another and see how this pans out."

Allie considered what he'd proposed. A tiny smile nipped at the corners of her mouth as she looked back at him, choosing her words carefully. "Yeah, maybe we could—take things slow, I mean."

Their eyes met, and she couldn't look away.

"Mom! Cam!" Ryan came running down the pier. He held up a gloved hand holding a large crab. "Look at this beaut!"

"Wow, honey."

Cam stepped closer, examined her son's catch. "Bet that's at least a seven-incher." He pulled out the little plastic tool from his back pocket and measured the crab from point-to-point. He shook his head. "Yup. Seven and a quarter. A definite keeper."

The look on Ryan's face mirrored Christmas morning. "Did you hear that, Mom? A keeper!"

Cam placed his hand on Ryan's shoulder. "So far, you have the biggest catch of the day." He helped him get the claw-snapping crustacean in the plastic bucket and secured the lid. "Okay, bait up and toss your ring out again."

Ryan busied himself fastening chicken to the bottom of the ring like he'd been shown. Cam knelt to help him.

Allie watched with a smile on her face. Her heart sped up again as she thought about Cam, about his sweetness and generosity and sense of humor—all qualities she admired.

He had a maturity she found very attractive. He was a few years older than she, but not by so much as to be an issue. Cam exhibited a stability she rarely saw in men, at least the ones she'd known. He seemed to know what he wanted, and wasn't interested in playing games to get it.

Clearly, he and Ryan had hit it off. Her kid had a way of smelling a fake from miles away. Cam truly liked her son and Ryan knew it.

She watched Cam help Ryan toss his crab ring over the railing on the pier. He patted her excited boy on the back before moving to the cooler, where he pulled out a Dr Pepper and handed it to Ryan before grabbing one for himself. He dug back in for another and held the can up to her.

She smiled and shook her head no.

Allie couldn't name the emotions she felt right then. A yearning sprouted, a longing as foreign as a small island country in the Pacific Rim. Long ago, she'd given up on having anyone in her life again—or, at least she'd put the notion on pause.

She let her mind wander into possibilities.

What would it be like to have someone to talk to—adult talk about adult things? To share victories and disappointments with someone who could be counted on to listen and understand?

It had been a long while since she'd had any physical contact with a man. What would it be like to be held in the dark? To smell a man next to her in bed, feel his arms against her skin and never worry about him ripping her heart apart by bringing another woman into that sacred place?

Of course, that was jumping far ahead. She and Cam hadn't even had a date yet.

Still, the thoughts left her shaky inside—and strangely excited.

Allie looked up. Several seagulls glided overhead, at first flapping their wings at fairly frequent intervals, but as the wind freshened, less and less frequently until at the height of their effort, they simply stopped flapping and soared.

Allie took in a deep breath.

The air was clear, the sky blue. Yet, in a single afternoon, everything had somehow changed.

12

The next morning dawned sunny and bright. All across Pacific Bay, families scurried from shop to shop, stopping to peer in windows filled with souvenir trinkets and pausing to admire brightly colored petunias cascading from hanging pots lining the sidewalks.

Allie watched the activity with interest. If she and Ryan got their house project done early, perhaps they could spend some time down at the beach later.

"Will that be all?" the clerk asked, smiling broadly at Allie. "Do you have all the paintbrushes you need?"

Allie nodded. "Yes, thanks." She opened her wallet and pulled out a couple of bills.

The clerk wiped his hands on his white apron and reached across the checkout counter. "I'm Bill Reynolds."

She shook his hand. "Allie Barrett."

"You're Tarver McIntosh's niece."

"Yes," she admitted, as she watched him ring up her purchase.

Mr. Reynolds shook his full head of gray hair. "Cleaning up Tarver's place must be a big job. I hope you've got some help.

What with your injuries and all. Everybody down at New Hope Church was praying when we heard of your little accident."

Her first thought was one of annoyance. She'd forgotten what it was like to live in a small town where everyone knew your business. In Ding Dong, you couldn't bake a cake without folks showing up to help you frost it.

Allie's conscience got the best of her. Her neighbors in Pacific Bay were concerned. They cared enough to pray for her. That was nothing to disdain.

She gave Mr. Reynolds a warm smile. "Thank you."

He handed her a receipt. "And you're spending time with Cameron Davis. Heard he took you and your boy crabbing. He's a fine man, that one. Lots of ladies in town are going to be disappointed to learn he's seeing someone."

"I—we're not *seeing* each other. I mean, we're friends. We—"

The old man grinned. "Well, whatever is going on, the whole town is rooting for you."

Allie didn't quite know what to say to that. She'd barely had time to digest the fact Cam might be interested in more than friendship. Now, it seemed, the notion was playing out in front of the whole town, like a film at the drive-in.

Allie tried to not let the smile slip from her face. Instead, she thanked Mr. Reynolds and made her way to the car, paint cans in hand.

Her phone buzzed on the way out to the car. When she answered, it was Ryan. "Mom! Captain Paul is going to let me help him inspect the bilge pumps. He says he's going to teach me how to check the lines. I won't be able to do any of this when I start school. I know I was supposed to help you, but would you care if—"

"You can stay and help Captain Paul." She grinned, hearing the excitement in her son's voice. She could use his help, but he needed time with good men, especially since his dad was out of the picture these days. "But stay out of the crew's way."

"Thanks, Mom! I love you."

"I love you too."

While summer vacation season would soon be drawing to a close, fishing remained in full swing. The passenger manifest had been full that morning. Captain Paul successfully maneuvered into a large school of Albacore tuna, delighting their guests by filling the boat's limit by noon.

Getting up hours before dawn each morning and working until late, then coming home to fill out paperwork and work the schedules for the coming weeks, in addition to cooking, cleaning, and doing laundry at the local laundromat left very little time for extra projects.

Her to-do list was long. The cottage shutters needed another coat of paint. A couple of boards on the deck were rotten and needed replaced. And her floors needed mopped. Despite having to tackle these projects on her own, this would be the perfect afternoon to do it.

After stopping for a few groceries on her way home from the hardware store, Allie unloaded the cans from her car and got right to work on the shutters.

First, she stripped the peeling paint from the weather-worn wood using a scraper. The process took several hours. Her injuries were nearly healed, but she still had to take things slow. By the time she finished, she could barely lift her arms.

She went inside for an aspirin and to get herself a glass of ice tea. She'd barely lifted the lid from the bottle of pain relievers when she heard an engine outside, like that of a motorcycle. She quickly tossed the tablets in her mouth and swallowed them down with a gulp of water before heading for the door to check out the source of the noise.

A brand new Harley was parked out front.

And sitting on the bike was someone she hadn't seen in a long while.

Allie's heart sunk. She swept her hand through her bangs "Oh, Lord, help me!" she said, eying the man climbing off the seat of the bike. "Deacon Ray. What are you doing here?"

He scrambled across the deck to meet her. "Well, hey!" He drew her into an unwanted hug.

She gently pushed him away. "I thought I had enough problems."

He grinned. "You saying you ain't glad to see me?" He rubbed at the back of his neck. "You know it's been a long time."

He tried to touch her cheek, but she dodged him. "Deacon Ray, I have ten dollars in my purse, and I don't even own a credit card." Both were true. Maybe not the entire truth, but that was certainly all she was going to reveal about her financial status.

"Now, Allie—do you think I'm here because I need money?"

She nodded, parked her hands on her hips. "Yes, I do."

He reached out and stroked her hair. "Well, you're wrong. I missed you."

She turned with a plaintive look. "What about Dixie? Or, Trixie? Or whatever her name was." She brushed past him, entered the house. He followed.

"Baby, c'mon. You know none of those girls meant a thing to me. You're the only girl I've ever really loved. You're my wife. I've really missed you," he said, in that weasel-like voice of his.

"*Was* your wife. We're divorced, remember?" Allie rolled her eyes and kept making her way to the kitchen. "God, I hope you're on your way to someplace else."

He grabbed her arm, turned her to face him.

"Well, I got some bad news. My daddy had a stroke. He's unresponsive and in a nursing home now. That's it—that's how he's going to go out of this world. A shriveled piece of his former self."

She softened, instantly feeling guilty. "Oh, no, Deacon Ray. I'm so sorry." His daddy had a lot of faults, but she knew Deacon Ray loved him.

Her ex-husband nodded. "Yup. He ate supper, climbed into bed, and just dropped to his knees." He snapped his fingers. "Just like that, the daddy I knew was gone. What was left was simply a hollow shell. You can see in his eyes, he just ain't there no more."

Allie filled with sympathy. She made a couple of steps toward him, went to pull her former husband into an awkward hug, then decided on a quick pat to the back instead. "I really am sorry. He was such a—" She paused, swallowed. "I know you loved him."

Deacon Ray lowered his head, then looked back up at her. "Yeah, won't be long before you and Ryan are all the family I got left." He moved for her, arms extended.

Allie quickly turned aside and bent to pull a weed growing up in her flower pot. "You have a strange way of defining family, especially since Ryan hasn't heard from you in so long. Where have you been, Deacon Ray?"

Out of the corner of her eye, she saw their son racing toward them on his bicycle. Allie braced herself for what she knew was coming.

Seconds later, Ryan burst cross the path toward them. "Hey, Mom. Whose motorcycle?" He caught sight of Deacon Ray, erupted into a full run. "Dad! He buried his head into Deacon Ray's middle, his arms wrapped firmly around his waist. "I can't believe you're really here!"

Deacon Ray's face broke into a wide smile. He lifted Ryan and swung him around. "Hey, buddy. Did you miss me?"

Ryan looked up at him and grinned. "Yeah. Did you miss me?"

Deacon Ray nodded. "Yeah, I sure did miss you, son."

Ryan leaned in, embraced his father's middle section so tightly Allie thought he might never let go. "Wow, Dad. It's really great to see you."

She watched the exchange for several seconds. Unable to help herself, her face finally broke into a tiny smile.

Ryan looked up at his dad. "Are you back? I mean, are you staying?"

Deacon Ray scruffed the top of his son's head with his knuckles. "Yeah, kid. I'm staying."

The smile instantly slid from Allie's face.

13

Allie gathered up the dirty dishes, balanced them on her forearm. "You get enough to eat, Ryan?"

Her son barely looked at her. "Yeah." He grinned over at Deacon Ray. "How about you, Dad?"

Deacon Ray leaned back in his chair, let out a belch. He rubbed his belly. "Best meal I've had in a long while. Allie, I'd forgotten how you could fry chicken!" He dabbed the corners of his mouth with a napkin, wadded it up, and tossed it onto his dirty plate.

"Well, like I was saying—" he cleared his throat. "After I put Dad in the nursing home, I had a bit of a wake-up call. I mean, no one is promised health forever, right? So, I decided to expand my horizons a bit. I left my job at that mechanic shop I worked for in Dallas and landed a gig at a fancy country club in Austin. Then those gawd-awful-hot summer months hit, and they lost a lot of bookings due to the heat. Didn't need a golf pro anymore." He rested the back of his head against his folded arms. "So, I got a wild hair and looked on the internet. Accepted me a job out in Salt Lake City selling lawn care services. Then winter hit, so I went to bartender school but—

well, not a lot of drinkers in Salt Lake City. I booked it up to Pacific Northwest. Heard it was really nice up there, and I thought, 'Well, what the heck—you only live once.' I just spent the past several months in Seattle working at a coffee shop." He glanced Allie's way. "You need an espresso with double-whip, and I'm your guy."

Allie looked at him with scorn. "So, you're broke, huh?"

Deacon Ray diverted his attention, leaned over and ruffled his son's hair. "Ryan, you're a string bean. I swear, you really shot up."

Allie coughed. "Yeah, and that string bean needs new pants every few months."

Ryan gave his mom a warning look. "You got a new leather jacket, Dad."

Deacon Ray grinned. "You like it?"

"Yeah, Dad. I do. And you got a new motorcycle too."

"Who wants dessert?" Allie interrupted, not bothering to hide her irritation.

Deacon Ray ignored her scowl. "Yup! It's the new Street Glide model. Your grandpa had a little money in the bank. Everybody down at the bar said the state of Texas would use it up for the ole man's care if I didn't spend it. So, figured I needed it worse than those fat cats in government. Besides, dad was a Navy vet and the people of this great nation owe him—not the other way 'round."

He reached for another biscuit before she whisked the basket off the table. "That bike leaves them all at the stoplight. It's faster than a waterslide coated in bacon grease."

Deacon Ray grew thoughtful. "Look, son, Someday, that bike will be yours. I had the attorney put that down in my papers and all. I mean, everything of mine, is yours. If I've learned nothing living this thing with my daddy, it's that we don't always have tomorrow. So, you have to make the very best of today. Know what I mean?"

Ryan nodded enthusiastically. "Make the best of today. Gotcha!"

Allie held back a heavy sigh and patted her son on the shoulder. "Honey, it's bedtime." She pulled Deacon Ray's plate from the table.

"Aw, Mom."

She gave her son a weak smile. "Sorry, bud. We've got to get up early."

Ryan glanced between them. "But—you are going to stay? Right, Dad?"

Deacon Ray rubbed his hands against the top of his legs. "Well, I'd like to."

Allie gave him another dirty look, rolled her eyes, and turned for the sink.

"Well, Allie—I'm kinda all moteled out."

"Bed, Ryan," Allie reminded.

Ryan rose from the table, pushed his chair in, and gave his dad a tight hug. "Goodnight, Dad. I love you." He slowly moved for the hallway, looking back over his shoulder, unable to tear his eyes from the table.

"Ryan," Allie called out. "There are other people in the room here."

Ryan lifted his shoulders in a guilty shrug. "Oh, sorry Mom." He returned, lifted onto his toes, and gave her a peck on the cheek. "G'night."

"Good night, buddy. Sweet dreams." She narrowed her eyes at her ex-husband, then swiped the ketchup bottle and the salt and pepper shakers from the table and headed for the cupboard.

Deacon Ray got up, timidly followed her. His hands were shoved deep in his pockets.

Allie grabbed the dishcloth, ran it under the sink. She brushed past him, returned to the table, and wiped the surface with wide, furious strokes.

Deacon Ray meandered to the table, pulled out his chair and sat back down. He steepled his fingers and watched her.

Allie circled the table, shoving in the remaining chairs. Without giving him a second look, she swept past him and headed for the living room.

She ran her hands through her hair, dropped to the sofa, and let out a heavy sigh, knowing full well what her conniving ex-husband was up to. His scheming had placed her in a horrible predicament. If Ryan woke and his dad was gone, she'd be the villain. Let Deacon Ray stay, and there was no telling where that road would lead. One thing she could count on—it would not be the highway to paradise.

She heard Deacon Ray get up from the table. She quickly busied herself gathering the cards Ryan had left out on the coffee table earlier.

Deacon Ray took a few tentative steps into the room, dug his hands in his pocket. "You know my daddy always said I was a fool to let you get away."

She looked up, annoyed. "He always knew how to call 'em."

"He pushed me to come after you more than once. I just kept telling him you needed time—to forgive me."

When she didn't respond, he reached and took both of her hands in his own. "He was right, Allie." He paused, looked deep in her eyes. "I was a fool."

"I'm not arguing. But shouldn't you be with him? I mean, do you think it was a good idea to leave your daddy all alone right now?"

Her ex-husband rubbed his forehead. "He would never have wanted me to sit by his bed watching him waste away." He got a firm look in his eyes. "Daddy would've wanted me to do exactly what I've done. And he would have been slapping his hat against his leg, happy I'd finally come to make amends. I mean, he knew we always loved each other."

She sighed, dropped her butt onto the sofa. "Well, it started out that way."

Deacon Ray sat on the coffee table, took one of her stocking feet in his hands, and started massaging the undersides of her feet with his fingers. "Remember the back seat of that old '57 Chevy?"

She examined her fingernails. "You mean the one that got repossessed?"

"Well, yeah." He brought her foot to his mouth, kissed her toes through her sock. "But while we had it, we sure used it."

She gawked at him, yanked her foot from his hands. "I was sixteen. I'm now in my thirties."

He shook his head. "Allie, I'm a different person."

She couldn't help but grin. "Yeah? Is that so? You know the Internal Revenue Service? Well, they were looking for you. Looks like you kind of forgot to file our income taxes—six years in a row!" She blew out the back door and onto the deck, letting the screen door slam in Deacon Ray's face.

"I've seen them, taken care of that," he told her, following her.

She parked her hands on her hips, whirled to face him. "Do you know how many bounced checks I had to cover?"

He grabbed her by the shoulders. "I'm a changed person."

"I don't believe you." She walked to the railing, stared out over the bay wishing she could throw her bum ex over and let the crabs have at him. If they liked rotten chicken, surely they'd take a shine to Deacon Ray.

"Ryan is real glad to see me, Allie."

She huffed as her gut twisted. "That's blackmail."

He stood behind her, far too close for her comfort. "If you can tell me the fire's out." He slipped his arms around her. "That there's not one tiny spark." He nestled his face against her ear. "Then I'll tip my hat and get back on my motorcycle."

Allie closed her eyes, smelled his aftershave, and felt her skin tingle, just like in the old days.

He kissed the soft spot behind her ear.

Shaken, she shoved him away. "Whatever you're trying to sell—the answer is no."

"Yeah, okay, sure," he said. "But you can't argue this isn't how you wanted things to go down."

"Sure. I didn't want to raise a kid alone, or clean up your financial messes either. But that's exactly what I faced when you couldn't keep your pants on." She flung the door open and went back into the house.

Deacon Ray followed close on her heels. He picked up his dirty plate off the kitchen table, moved to the sink and ran it under some water, flicked some of the food particles off with his fingers. "I—I can sleep in Ryan's bed. Or on the floor in his room," he told her over his shoulder.

Allie frowned and took the dish from him. "I haven't said you could stay." She grabbed the generic bottle of dish soap off the window sill, squeezed a generous amount into the sink.

He playfully bumped her with his shoulder. "But you never said I can't."

Allie slammed the water off in the faucet. "Dang it, Deacon Ray! Why'd you have to go and ruin everything? Why couldn't you be who I thought you were when I married you?"

He picked up the dishcloth, started washing the dishes. "Well, I'm going to be. You'll see." He paused. "I want to do this for you—and for Ryan. He needs his father."

She stomped to the counter, grabbed the plate of cookies left over from dinner and tossed them one-by-one into the bag, letting what he said sit there on her all heavy, like one of those bloated old seals down on the dock. A picture formed in her mind, the image of Ryan's face when he first saw his dad, of them clinging to one another. She conjured the worried look he gave her as he trudged off to bed.

There was no arguing the fact she'd eat shards of glass for that boy.

Scowling, she turned to face Deacon Ray, square on. "Listen up! You need to understand this is only going to be temporary. Just a visit." She pointed into the living room. "You get the sofa. We only have one bathroom, and I use it first."

14

Morning rumbled in with a distant clap of thunder, putting an end to Allie's sleepless night. She rose from her rumpled bed and opened the window. A brisk, easterly wind blew into the room, carrying the scent of briny sea air heavy with impending rain.

Apparently, the days of sunshine were over.

She sighed, knowing there would be some disappointed tourists when they learned their fishing trip would be canceled due to inclement weather. Allie mourned the loss of income—even more, she found herself lamenting the fact she had an ex-husband on her sofa she wasn't exactly sure what to do with.

Allie wandered out to the kitchen to put the coffee on, then headed for Ryan's room. On the way, she stopped in the living room, pushed at the lump hidden under the covers. "You might want to get up. This household doesn't sleep the day away. We have a lot of chores to tend to."

Deacon Ray slowly peeked out from under the wadded blanket, looked at her with one barely open eye. He pushed himself to a sitting position, yawned. "Goodness sakes, what time is it? The sun ain't even up yet."

"Doesn't matter. We have work to do." She didn't belabor the point. Instead, she continued down the hallway. She'd wake Ryan and then make them all breakfast before heading down to the marina.

Her son bounced right out of bed the minute she nudged him awake. "Is Dad here? He didn't leave, did he?"

"No, he's still here."

Ryan scrambled into his jeans and pulled a shirt over his head.

"Uh, that one's dirty. Let's get a clean one," she told him, pointing to the open drawer.

He pulled a clean shirt on, tossed the dirty T-shirt to the floor in the direction of his hamper. "This okay?" he asked, turning so she could inspect his new choice.

She nodded.

Without another word, Ryan scrambled down the hall. "Hey, Dad! How about we go fishing today?"

"Well, looks like the storm is going to foil any fishing plans. But maybe we could buy some rain gear and take a drive up the coast on my bike."

Allie darted down the hall and wedged herself between them. "No, huh-uh. My kid is not going to ride that bike. Period —end-of-story!" She jutted a pointed finger at her ex-husband. "I mean it."

He held up hands in surrender. "Okay, I got you." He looked over at his son. "She always this cranky in the mornings?"

She huffed. "And, just because it's raining doesn't mean it's not a workday. Ryan needs to help out on the boat." She gave Deacon Ray a pointed look. "I could use your help too."

"Boat?"

Ryan pulled his dad's shirt off the back of the sofa and handed it to him. "Yeah, we own a boat. A big one."

Deacon Ray turned his attention to Allie while pulling his shirt on. "That so?"

She cringed. Her business was her own, and she wasn't exactly excited to have her ex-husband prying his nose into her affairs. "*Reel Time* was my uncle's boat," she explained. "A commercial fishing operation is a lot of work—*hard* work from before the sun is up until sundown. Doesn't leave a lot of free time to play."

Hoping she'd made her point, and more importantly, diffused any notion Deacon Ray might entertain hanging around to share in her good fortune, Allie drilled her ex with a look to anchor her point. "Work that you'll have to share in. Consider yourself a temporary houseguest who is earning his room and board for the *short* time you're here."

His eyebrows lifted. "I get you. But I was kind of thinking since I hadn't been in this part of the world, I might take a day and sightsee before buckling down and focusing on work." He turned to Ryan. "We could borrow your mom's car. I read there's a big oyster farm right down the bay. Maybe we could cop some of those bad boys and put them on the BBQ tonight with butter and Tabasco." He grinned. "You know what they say about oysters? They're an aphrodisiac."

Ryan frowned. "What's an aphrodisiac?"

Allie quickly interrupted. "Never mind. No one's going to the oyster farm. Like I said, we all have work to do—on the boat."

The guys both groaned, but one look from her and neither elected to argue the point further.

Allie hurried and cooked breakfast, pancakes made in the shape of crabs—Ryan's new favorite. When they'd finished eating, she told Ryan to go wash his face and hands while she cleaned up.

She half expected Deacon Ray to hang in the kitchen and cause her grief. Thankfully, he didn't. In fact, she wasn't sure where he'd gone, but wherever it was, he'd left his blankets in a rumpled mess on the sofa.

She groaned inside. *I am not his mother*, she reminded herself while folding the items. She headed for the hall closet, carrying the bedding, past the open bathroom door.

She stopped at the open bathroom door to tell Ryan to get a move-on. Inside, Deacon Ray climbed into the shower, but not before she got a full-view glimpse of his bare backside.

She quickly squeezed her eyes shut, opened her mouth to scold him for not closing the door.

If he was going to stay a night or two, there had to be rules!

Before she could form words, he peeked out from the shower curtain. "Ha, caught you looking."

Allie growled. "I wasn't— Uh, I did not look." She launched into a lecture about being considerate of others. He wasn't the only one in this house and he needed to be dressed when not in bed and asleep.

Deacon Ray simply laughed and turned the water on.

IGNORING THE OMINOUS SKY OVERHEAD, Allie shoved a bucket and some rags into Deacon Ray's hands. "Here, take this. The latrine needs scrubbed."

"The latrine?"

"Yeah, you know—the little toilet behind that door in the cabin. This boat doesn't clean itself."

Deacon Ray looked at her with disbelief. "Somebody woke up on the wrong side of the bed."

Allie threw him a dirty look. He shrugged and took the bucket. "Where is this latrine thing?"

She pointed. "In there." Her arms went around Ryan's shoulders. "C'mon, we need to organize the tackle."

For the next half hour, they all worked at their assigned tasks without conversation. The jigs, the treble hooks, and minnow lures were all sorted and stored in their proper spots.

The deck was mopped and hosed down. The glass windows sprayed with cleaner and wiped spotless.

Deacon Ray popped his head out the door. "Houston, we've got a problem," he announced.

"What kind of problem?" Allie dropped her box of weights on the floor of the deck.

He shrugged. "Not sure, but looks like the toilet is stopped up."

She brushed past him, horrified to find water seeping out from under the door. "Deacon Ray! What happened?"

"How do I know?"

Allie looked at the situation helplessly. "Well, can't you fix it?"

"I don't know how to fix the thing. I mean, I can't very well — That water is nasty."

She raced to the tool locker looking for a plunger. Finding none, she returned and barked, "Stay here! And don't touch a thing!"

"What's going on, Mom?"

"Stay with your Dad. I'll be right back." She bolted across the deck, climbed down the boarding plank and onto the pier, then raced in the direction of the Search and Rescue boat, hoping to find Cameron.

As luck would have it, she spotted him wearing his bright orange vest. She waved her arms and called out to him. "Cam! Hey, Cam."

His head popped up when he heard her voice. Without hesitation, he scaled the bridgeway and jogged over to meet her. "What's up? Everything okay?"

"I need—uh, sorry." She bent over her legs to catch her own breath. "Not an emergency, or anything. My latrine is flooding, and I don't know how to stop it."

"Ah, the raw water seacock for the head might not be open."

"The what?" she asked.

"Never mind. Wait here," he said, then sprinted back to the SAR boat. Seconds later, he reappeared carrying a red toolbox. "Okay, let's go."

The sky opened, and it started to rain, drenching both of them as they hurried for her boat. Midway, Cam stopped, pulled off his vest and held it over her head as a makeshift umbrella.

Onboard, Deacon Ray and Ryan were sitting at a table in the cabin playing Yahtzee. Ryan leaned over and examined the dice. "Should I take my sevens?"

Deacon Ray didn't answer. Instead, he took a drink from his soda can and sized-up Cam. "You the hired hand?"

"Nah, just a friend," Cam answered as he followed Allie. "Here to help out."

Deacon Ray left the table, trailed after them as they made their way through the cabin. "I'm the husband."

"Husband?" She heard the confusion in Cam's voice.

Before she could turn and explain, Deacon Ray added, "We got divorced a while back."

"Wouldn't that make you the ex-husband?" Cam challenged.

She pulled on Cam's arm. "I'll explain later. Right now, I've got a latrine spilling water all over."

Cam set his toolbox down, rolled up his shirt sleeves and bent for a better look. "Don't worry. We'll get this under control," he assured her as he squeezed into the tiny space and got to work.

"Well, if you don't need my help..." Deacon Ray backed away.

"Yeah, we got it," Allie told him, not bothering to hide her annoyance.

Twenty minutes later, Cam closed his tool box. "Well, that should do it." He backed out of the latrine, rolled his sleeves back down, and buttoned his cuffs before looking past her. He nodded toward Deacon Ray. "So, you have an ex visiting?"

"It's only temporary," she offered as an explanation. "He's Ryan's father. It'd been a while and Ryan was pretty thrilled to see him." She shrugged, trying to appear nonchalant. "Deacon Ray, that's his name, well—he's out of work and had no place to stay. But, it's only temporary," she repeated.

"Yup, times are tough," he said, his eyes thoughtful.

She stared at the cleaning rag in her hand. "Like I said, Ryan and his daddy. Well, it's important to my boy," she said, defensively. "That's the only reason he's here." She dared to look up.

Cam didn't say anything.

Outside, a thunderclap exploded. Allie nearly jumped out of her skin. The sound startled Cam as well. Even so, he held her gaze. "You might want to get a mop. I'll help you get this mess cleaned up."

When everything was finally back in order, they made their way back out to the galley.

"Yahtzee!" Deacon Ray shouted and threw his arms up in victory.

"No way." Ryan leaned over and examined the dice, disappointment written across his face.

"Yes, way." Deacon Ray scooped up a pen, made a big X in the appropriate box on the scorecard.

Cam examined the sky through the porthole window. "Well, toilet's all fixed. Looks like someone tossed a couple of paper towels down."

Allie turned to her son. "Ryan, you know better!"

"But, Mom. I didn't do it."

Deacon Ray quickly scooped up the dice and boxed up the game pieces, slid the lid back on the box. "Well, the rain has stopped," he stammered. "I guess we should be getting on home before it starts up again."

Allie's hands squeezed into fists at her side. She held her tongue, turned to Cameron. "Look, I really appreciate you saving the day. Would you let me pay you back? Come to dinner?"

He lifted his brows. "Depends." He glanced over at Deacon Ray. "I suppose I could be talked into staying in town for dinner. What are you serving?"

"Fried chicken." She parked her hands on her hips, his meaning seeping in. "And mashed potatoes and homemade milk gravy." She rushed to add, "And for dessert—uh, marionberry cobbler topped with Tillamook vanilla ice cream."

Deacon Ray glanced between them, scowled. "We had chicken last night."

She glowered back in his direction. "And we're having it again." She launched the words with enough force to put a hole in his argument.

Her ex-husband lifted his open palms in mock surrender. "Okay, got it. No problem."

Cam watched the exchange. His face drew into a slow smile. "I love fried chicken. I accept."

15

By evening, the storm had moved out, leaving the sky smelling fresh and the water's surface in the bay rising and falling with rhythmic ease. The sun was gone now, and the remaining clouds on the horizon had turned twilight blue.

Allie typically loved standing on the deck outside the little house, taking in the wonder of it all. But tonight, she couldn't make the time. She had a dinner guest coming.

She raced around the kitchen, wishing she'd suggested a meal that didn't take so much preparation. Fried chicken was one of her few specialties, but dredging the pieces through flour and dropping the legs and thighs into spitting hot oil had left her counter a mess. Never mind what her hair must look like.

She glanced in her reflection in the kitchen window just as a knock came at the door.

"I'll get it," Ryan called out.

Allie sighed, tucked a stray strand of hair back in place, and wiped her hands on a kitchen towel as she made her way into the living room.

Deacon Ray reclined on the couch, his head wedged on the crook of his bent elbow and his stocking feet propped against the back of the sofa. She popped him with the towel. "Get up."

"But *Wheel of Fortune* is still on."

Ignoring his protest, she joined Ryan as he opened the front door.

Cameron held out a bouquet of flowers. "Dahlias," he said. "Homegrown."

The gesture made Allie smile. "They're lovely. Let me get them into a vase of water."

Deacon Ray scrambled from the sofa, ran his fingers through his hair. "Aren't those the same flowers we had at our wedding?"

It took great effort not to roll her eyes. "Not even a little."

Deacon Ray nodded. "Oh, that's right. We had those daisies. Your favorite."

"Well, they were," she conceded. "Tastes change. A few years ago, I realized daisies can be infested with aphids."

She filled a mason jar with water and arranged the brightly colored blooms, placed them in the middle of the kitchen table. She smiled over at Cam. "Hope you're hungry."

"I sure am," he said, rubbing his hands together.

Allie paused, taking in the sight of him—details she'd barely noticed before. His strong shoulders and lean hips, his green eyes and how his square jaw set off a full, masculine mouth. He wore jeans and a denim button-down shirt and exuded self-confidence. Cameron Davis knew who he was and didn't try to impress anybody.

Even more, he smelled like cedar and fresh grass, with a hint of the laundry soap her mama used to use.

She tried to keep her voice strong and steady. "Would you like something to drink?"

"What do you have?"

She opened the refrigerator door. "Milk or beer?"

"Milk."

Deacon Ray slid into a chair, scooted close to the table. "I like beer."

Allie wedged a can of beer, the milk carton, and a bottle of salad dressing in her arm and kicked the door closed with her foot. "Yes, I know."

"You can sit by me," she told Cam, directing him to a spot at the table.

Ryan took his napkin and laid it carefully over his lap like she'd taught him. "You're in for a treat, Cam. Mom makes the best fried chicken. When I say the best, I mean it. The best!"

Deacon Ray took the can of beer, popped the top before directing his attention at Cam. "I know we've met, but we haven't been properly introduced." He extended his hand across the small table. "Deacon Ray Barrett."

Cam shook his hand. "Cameron Davis."

Allie watched the exchange as she delivered the platter of fried chicken to the table. "Hope you guys are hungry. I think I may have overcooked a bit. There's enough for twenty people. I seem to always do that—cook too much, I mean. I take after my mama."

Deacon Ray slipped a fried leg onto his plate, then went for another. "Well, Cameron Davis. You seem to be a pretty handy fellow to have around. Even carry around your own toolbox."

Cameron placed his napkin on his lap. "I tinker a bit." He glanced around the table as Allie took her seat. "Anyone mind if I say the blessing?"

"Sure, that'd be great," Allie told him.

They all bent their heads.

"Bless us, oh Lord, and these thy gifts which we are about to receive from thy bounty. And bless the hands that prepared this delicious meal we're about to eat. Amen."

Allie's heart swelled. That was the same blessing her mama used to say before meals.

Deacon Ray smoothed his mustache. "So, you say you tinker a lot. What do you do? For a living, I mean?" He grabbed the bowl of mashed potatoes and scooped a mound onto his plate, then passed the bowl on to Ryan.

"I co-own a breakfast diner with my father—the Pig 'n' Pancake located downtown. But I spend my days working Search and Rescue."

Ryan nodded with enthusiasm. "Yeah, that's the Coast Guard. Isn't that right, Cam?"

Cam smiled over at him. "Yup, that's right."

Jealousy clouded Deacon Ray's expression. He took a swig of his beer. "Just like in the movies, huh? I mean, kinda like Kevin Costner or—" He snapped his fingers. "Ryan, who's that dude who played in the *The Fast and the Furious*?"

Ryan shrugged. "I don't know. I'm too young to see that one."

"Vin Diesel. Yeah, you're a guy like him—a hero of sorts." Deacon Ray drew a chicken leg to his mouth, took a big bite and chewed. "A real man." He waited for Cam's reaction to his obvious needling.

Allie nervously glanced between the two. This dinner was a bad idea.

Before she could intercept the conversation and maneuver matters to safer ground, Cam slowly smiled. "Yeah, some might consider me a tough guy. But I also write haiku, can paint a fair sunset using alcohol ink, and I have learned the skills required to rescue people in trouble. Especially damsels in distress."

Allie nearly spit her food onto his plate. "Those are definitely useful skills."

Deacon Ray salted his potatoes, then scooped a dollop of gravy over the top. "I'm pretty good with damsels myself."

Cam glanced over at Allie, winked. "I heard."

16

Allie invited Cam for dinner several more times over the following week.

On Monday, she caught him trolling past the *Reel Time,* coming into the bay on the SAR boat. She stood on the deck and waved her arms wildly. "Want to come to dinner? We're having something simple. Just wieners and sauerkraut, but you're welcome to join us," she shouted.

On Wednesday, she served meatloaf. He slathered a large slice with ketchup and claimed it was the best he'd ever eaten.

On Thursday, he brought over some orange roughy and taught her how to poach the fish filets in white wine and lemon. That time, it was her turn to rave.

By Friday morning, Deacon Ray had had enough. Allie was mopping the kitchen floor in her bare feet when he entered. He wore jeans and a Seattle Mariners T-shirt, no shoes. "Hey, can I talk to you about something?"

"Uh, don't step on my wet floor."

He jumped back, frowned. "Yeah, how come that Cameron fellow always finishes up at the Coast Guard and strolls by your boat down at the marina right before we're heading home for dinner? How come he always ends up with his feet under our dinner table?"

"*My* dinner table," she corrected. "And to answer your question, I think he plans it that way."

AFTER DINNER ON FRIDAY NIGHT, Deacon Ray pushed his chair back from the table. "Well, Allie. You outdone yourself on that lasagna. That was pretty tasty. Garlic bread was good too." He turned to Cam. "She knows that's my favorite."

Allie stood, began clearing the table.

"No, ma'am. Here, let me." Deacon Ray rushed to her side, pulled the nearly empty lasagna pan from her hands. "I'll take care of this." He motioned for Ryan to help him. "Let's say we get this kitchen cleaned for your mom and then we'll challenge those two to a game of poker."

Allie shook her head. "Oh, I don't think—"

"Nonsense. The boy's got to learn to play. A man's not a man unless he knows the difference between Texas Hold 'Em and Seven-card stud." He placed the lasagna pan by the sink. "I may not be able to sew, but I've won my share at the table."

Ryan's eyes lit up. "Sounds fun, Dad."

Allie pondered how to shut down the idea when Cam spoke up. "You know, much as I'd like to join in, I'm going to have to pass. My dad's birthday is coming up and I wanted to shop for him a gift." He looked over at Allie, reached, and touched her hand. "You're welcome to join me."

"Sure, I'd like to—"

Deacon Ray flipped around. "That's a great idea. You know, my boy had a birthday recently. We need to go get you a gift, right buddy?"

Ryan's eyes lit up. "Sure, Dad!"

Disappointment immediately flooded Allie. "Oh, okay."

"Yes, come on along," Cam told them, looking like he could easily spatter Deacon Ray's sugar if he had a mind to. "More the merrier."

Allie looped her arm with his, leaned close. "Thanks. You're a good sport."

Cam drove them to a shop located on Highway 101 which was the main thoroughfare through town and the road travelers took if they were driving north to Astoria or south to Bandon. The shop was owned by a friend of his and had been in business for over twenty years.

The proprietor's name was Susan Wilson. She welcomed them as soon as they stepped inside the door. "Where've you been keeping yourself, Cameron Davis?" She turned to Allie. "This man has missed more Bunco nights in the past two months than in the prior two years." Her eyes held a hint of suggestion.

"I'm Susan," she said, taking Allie's hand in her own. "And you must be the sweet girl who moved in to take over her uncle's place." She glanced at Deacon Ray, smiled warmly. "That house was a real mess. Everyone in town is talking about how she fixed the place up. That's not all. She's earned a lot of admiration in these parts. It takes a lot of guts to take on a commercial fishing boat and make a go of it." Clearly, she admired Allie and her efforts.

Her flattery had Allie laughing and blushing at the same time. She gave the woman's hand a squeeze, knowing she'd found a friend.

"Mom, can I go check out the electronics?" Ryan inclined his head toward the back of the store.

"I'll go with him." Deacon Ray put his hand on Ryan's shoulder, and off they went, chattering about operating systems and circuit boards.

Cam asked Susan if she could show him some Pendleton shirts. Allie learned the shirts were made of wool and produced in an Oregon town of the same name. The apparel was Muncy's favorite.

"We just got in a new shipment," Susan told him. "Make sure and look at that teal-blue one. It's a *beaut!*"

Cam ended up buying the one Susan recommended. She gift-wrapped the box. "I like to provide a little extra service to reward people who shop here. I think that's the reason competition from online retailers hasn't shuttered our doors."

"Nor will they," Cam assured her. "Neighbors take care of neighbors."

Ryan rushed up the aisle toward the checkout counter. "Mom, look what Dad bought me!" He held up a box. "An Apple Watch!"

Allie scowled. "Oh, honey. That's far too extravagant." She took hold of Deacon Ray's arm and dragged him aside. "You should have talked with me first. Ryan's too young to have such an expensive item. Besides that, I am not inclined to pay a monthly fee." She didn't bother asking how he'd paid for it. A credit card perhaps, a bill he'd skip out on eventually if history was any indicator.

"You don't have to pay an additional monthly charge as long as he pairs it with your phone," he argued. "Let me do something nice for him—something special. I'm his dad."

Allie folded. How could she argue when Deacon Ray was trying to make Ryan happy?

She sighed in resignation. "Okay, but next time please check with me first."

"Thanks, Al." Deacon Ray drew her into an embrace.

Over his shoulders, Allie's eyes met Cam's. She grimaced and quickly pulled away. "Yeah, okay."

Outside, the parking lot was now dark except for the lights on the poles. They made their way to Cam's truck. In the back seat, Ryan opened the box with excitement, and he and Deacon Ray synced the watch with Allie's phone and chose the settings.

"Do you like it, son?" Deacon Ray sounded as excited as Ryan.

Ryan threw his arms around his dad. "Oh, yes! I really do."

The scene made Allie's heart grow warm. Deacon Ray had many faults, but he was Ryan's dad, and he was trying.

As their marriage had dissolved—and for good reason—she'd often worried about the emotional impact the split would have on her precious son. She knew from all the books she'd read on the subject that the changes and uncertainty could have a negative effect. Everything inside her wanted to lessen the blow and the potential for him to feel the split was in any way his fault.

She still remembered the night she'd had to sit Ryan down on the edge of his bed to explain what was happening.

"But who will be my daddy now?" he'd asked, his eyes filling with tears.

Allie scooped him next to her chest, kissed the top of his sweaty head. "Your dad will always be your dad, baby. We just won't be living in the same house anymore."

She closed her eyes now, took in the excitement in their voices. She could find many reasons to send Deacon Ray on down the road—only one of which was the man sitting in the driver's seat next to her. Her heart longed to be free of the baggage. She needed to move on and build a new life for herself, and for Ryan. Free of Deacon Ray.

Yet, the look on her son's face stopped her.

There would be time to send her ex packing—but that moment wasn't now. Not when Ryan was so happy.

What kind of mother would pull the scab off her little boy's emotional wound?

Allie looked across at Cam, studying his face. "You're awfully quiet."

Cam turned his truck onto the gravel landing outside her house. Across the bay, the sun had already begun to set. "I'm good," he told her. She suspected he was doing his best to take in the situation and be a good sport about all this. She appreciated that about him. Still, it was a lot to ask.

He put the truck in park, switched off the engine. They all climbed out of the truck.

Cam hung back as they made their way to the front door. "Hey, Deacon Ray. Let's you and me have a little talk."

Deacon Ray looked up with surprise. "Don't you want to go inside first?"

"Nah, let's talk out here," Cam said, digging his hands inside his jean pockets.

Allie grew concerned. "Everything okay?"

Cam nodded. "We'll be in in a minute."

Allie hesitated, then placed her hand on Ryan's shoulder. "All right. We'll be inside."

When the front door closed, the two men made their way out on the deck. Deacon Ray stared up at the starry night sky. "So, what's up?"

Cam slowly turned. "Mister, I wasn't going to speak in front of your boy, but that box didn't match the watch inside."

Deacon Ray looked like a deer caught in the headlights. "What? I don't understand what you're saying."

Cam's eyes narrowed. "Oh, I think you do. You switched boxes to lower the price you'd pay. In these parts, we call that stealing."

Deacon Ray shrugged. "Yeah, well—the lady wasn't actually out anything. She just didn't make any profit on the sale."

A seal's deep bark drifted from across the bay. Cam grabbed Deacon Ray's wrist. "Well, like I said—that's called being a thief." He looked at him full-on. "Tell you what—I'm going to cut you a break. Tomorrow, you're going to go back into that store and tell my friend, Susan, that you discovered the situation when you got home. You're going to hand her the difference and make things right. Agreed?"

Deacon Ray pulled his arm back and tried to smile. "Don't go getting all hot under the collar. Sure, I'll do that. It's not that big a deal." His eyes searched Cam's. "Okay? We're good?"

Cam didn't respond. Instead, he nodded toward the door. "We'd better get inside." He paused. "And Deacon Ray?"

"Yeah?"

Cam gave him a sharp look. "Another stunt like that and it'll be time to cut this visit short."

17

After dinner, Allie walked Cam out, leaving Deacon Ray with clear instructions to finish cleaning the kitchen and Ryan being told he needed to brush his teeth and get ready for bed.

At the car, she crossed her arms and cleared her throat. "Tell me, what was that all about when you took Deacon Ray outside?"

Cam's gaze scrolled past her to the marina in the distance "Let's just say we cleared up a little misunderstanding."

She stared at the dim lights from the windows of the cottages along the pier shone on dozens of boats, their empty masts poking in the air. "Deacon Ray may not win any Man of the Year awards, but he's the only daddy Ryan has."

Cam slowly nodded. His eyes narrowed. "A boy needs his father."

"It's not fair to keep them separated. I mean, just because our marriage ended doesn't mean I can keep Ryan from his dad. If Deacon Ray came all this distance and wants to spend time with his son, who am I to stand in the way of that?"

Cam looked at her long and hard. "You're a good mother."

"Exactly! I mean, what kind of mother tries to keep a wedge of distance between her kid and his father? Sure, I wish Deacon Ray had a few more qualities worth emulating, but I don't get to tell him he can't spend time with Ryan. Ryan deserves a relationship with his dad, and I don't want to get in the way of that. He'd grow up and end up hating me for it."

Her mouth was hemorrhaging. She needed to take a breath, stop talking.

As if reading her thoughts, Cam studied her. "I suppose the real question is whether Deacon Ray needs to build a relationship with his son while sleeping on your sofa."

If truth were a target, he'd hit a bull's-eye. The words stung.

She tried to hide her discomfiture. "I know what it looks like, Cam. But his stay is only temporary. Trust me. Deacon Ray never camps in a situation for long. I've lost count of how many relationships, jobs, commitments he's moved on from after getting bored with his circumstances. I promise, it won't be long, and he'll be packing up and moving on. Until then, I owe it to my boy to foster this time with his dad."

Cam let her words dangle in the salty air for several seconds before responding. "Perhaps. But that dining table of yours is getting a bit crowded."

His words, and the meaning behind them, weaseled their way inside her heart. Feeling defensive, she diverted her gaze and pointed to his left hand. "You're one to talk. I mean, you still wear a wedding ring."

She immediately regretted deflecting the conversation in that manner. She'd crossed a line and was sorry.

Before she could say so, Deacon Ray burst through the door.

"Hey, you two!" He trotted toward them. "Ryan and I were just talking. There's that arcade down on the boardwalk and I want to take him—and the two of you—my treat." He waited expectantly. "So, what do you say? Shall we go?"

A wave washed the shoreline, nearly drowning his voice.

"C'mon. It'll be fun," he added, a little louder this time.

Cam stepped closer—so close she felt the warmth of his flesh. He reached in the dark and let his fingers brush against hers, ever so slightly, a touch heavy with meaning.

"Sure," Cam said, barely tearing his gaze from her. "Sounds great."

DEACON RAY STEPPED up to the ticket window. "Three adults. One junior," he told the young blonde sitting behind the glass. He winked at her and slid a crisp one-hundred-dollar bill through the slot and into her waiting hands.

She cracked her gum. "You're going to love the new *Dance Revolution* attraction." She waited for the tickets to spit out of her machine and handed them to him. Scaffolded breasts spilled from her low-cut neckline.

"Good to hear," he told her, grinning like a teenager in heat.

"Dad, are we going to get some cotton candy?"

Deacon Ray reluctantly pulled his attention from the window and passed out the tickets. "Of course. And some chocolate-covered raisins and salt water taffy."

Cam's hand went to Allie's back, guiding her as they followed Deacon Ray and Ryan into the arcade.

"Let's ride the Tilt-A-Whirl." Ryan darted for some empty seats.

"Oh, I don't know," Allie told him. "I feel my eyes cross when I ride anything that spins."

Deacon Ray slung his arm across her shoulder. "You're not chicken, are you?"

She sighed and rolled her eyes. "No, not chicken. I just don't like feeling dizzy." She slipped out from under his unwanted arm and tentatively climbed into the cart, slid in next to Ryan." She waved at Cam to join her. "C'mon."

He shook his head. "Not my thing."

Deacon Ray opened his mouth to respond. The look on Cam's face seemed to make him change his mind.

Her ex climbed in next to her. "Well, I'm definitely in." He reached and helped them all in.

Allie's heart began to pound as she questioned her sanity. Why had she consented to this nonsense?

"Don't be afraid, Mom." Ryan grinned widely. "This ride's going to be a blast."

She closed her eyes and focused. Overhead, music nearly drowned out the sound of laughter and the dinging of a pinball machine in the distance.

Her palms turned a bit damp as she tightly grasped the safety bar. A click and she was harnessed in place. She heard the whoosh of air brakes releasing, sensed movement.

Allie pasted a tight smile across her face when the tiny car jerked forward, stopped again as attendants loaded the next car...and the next. Chains ground beneath, and their car chugged forward. Her senses went on high alert as the car spun slowly to the left, then rocked to the right.

The smell of corndogs, sweet cotton candy, and buttered popcorn filled the air. These aromas hit her nostrils, but instead of feeling hungry, Allie's stomach lurched in anticipation of what was ahead.

Far too soon, the lyrical music seemed to fade, signaling the ride was about to begin in earnest. Suddenly, her line of vision blurred. It was as if the cart they were in was suspended from invisible strings. Her heart pounded, and she held her breath, knowing what was about to happen.

She opened her eyes as the tip of their cart took its first serious dip. The motion sent the cart spinning to the right. A second dip spun the cart in the opposite direction. Her stomach followed suit.

Allie tightened her grip on the bar as Cam's image whirred past.

"Let's make it go faster!" Ryan hollered.

"No!" Allie protested. But it was too late. Deacon Ray's body shifted against her, squishing her into Ryan. The transfer of weight created an imbalance that propelled the cart into a spinning motion that lifted her stomach into her throat. She became dizzy and unable to focus as colors blurred together.

Deacon Ray laughed.

Allie squeezed her eyes shut again. She held her breath and counted backward. It was all she could do to keep from panicking as the cart spun back and forth and went around and around for what seemed like forever.

Finally, the ride slowed.

She released her breath slowly, opened her eyes. Beside her, Deacon Ray beamed. On her other side, Ryan had grown quiet. "You okay, sweetie?" she barely eked.

"Of course, he's okay. He's my kid!" Deacon Ray leaned out of the pink-canopied cart and waved to the attendant. "We'll go again."

The attendant folded his arms against the waist of his red apron. "Sorry, there's a line." He pointed to the people waiting to take their turn.

Deacon Ray shrugged. "Dang. Well, whatever." He waited for the release click and then pushed the retention bar forward. He climbed out. Allie and Ryan followed.

Cam gave them a wave. She walked in his direction on shaky legs.

Cam folded his arms across his chest and smiled. "So, how was the ride?"

"Don't ask," she told him. "I think my stomach is still back in that cart."

He turned to her son. "What about you, Ryan? Have fun?"

She noticed her son's face had paled. "You okay, honey?"

He wrapped his arms around his stomach. "Not really," he admitted. "That ride made my tummy hurt."

Deacon Ray rushed up. "You ready to go again, son?" He pointed across the arcade. "What do you say we try the bumper cars?"

Ryan glanced between Allie and Deacon Ray. "I—I think I'm too young to drive."

"Not on the bumper cars, you're not." Deacon Ray pulled at Ryan's arm. "C'mon. Let's go."

She watched Deacon Ray drag Ryan away and hand the attendant their tickets.

"What?" Cam asked, seeing the look on her face.

She let out a sigh. "At times, it feels like I have two kids."

Laughing, Cam took her hand. "C'mon."

"Where are we going?"

"It's our turn. There's a candy store next door. The best saltwater taffy you've ever tasted. And popcorn balls."

She grinned back at him. "Cotton candy?"

He nodded. "And caramel apples."

"Wait here." She jogged over to where Deacon Ray and Ryan were climbing into their bumper cars, told them where she'd be.

She rejoined Cam, slipped her hand back into his. "Okay, sure. Let's go."

Minutes later, they were huddled on a metal bench sitting in comfortable silence, eating cotton candy, and looking out over the surf. In the dusk of night, the waves were barely discernable but for the gently roaring sound as the tide rolled in.

"You know, I'd wanted something different," Allie said, more wistfully than she'd intended. She paused, licked some of the sweet concoction stuck to her fingers. "A marriage different than what my parents had."

Allie thought about how her mama stayed with her daddy, even when his drinking got out of hand and he started borrowing from the church funds. She stayed even when the elders were forced to remove him from the pulpit and he flitted from one no-good job to another, never able to make ends meet. "There's not a lot of good-paying jobs for a pastor marched out of the pulpit," her mama claimed, defending him. Never mind he somehow still found money for his bad habit.

Not that her daddy was a bad man. Her father loved her, and he loved her mama—right up until the very end. An end brought on by his diabetes. Low insulin and high levels of vodka didn't mix very well.

By then, Mama was sick too. She died of malignant breast cancer, the kind that would have been beatable had she had insurance and gone to the doctor. When Allie learned of the situation and finally convinced her to be checked, it was too late.

Allie squinted her eyes, trying to focus on the sound of the waves crashing against the sand. "When I buried my mama, Deacon Ray was the only family I had left, except for the uncle in Oregon who I'd never even met. And Ryan, of course." She tugged a tuft of cotton candy from the bag, rolled it in between her fingers. "I accepted far too much for far too long. Guess I was afraid to let go."

Cam turned pensive, his eyes distant. "I agree. It's not easy."

"What about you?" she asked. "You were married. What did you hope for?"

"Longer," he said thoughtfully.

"What do you mean?"

He took her hand and squeezed. "I'd simply wanted longer."

"Mom! There you are." Ryan sprinted over and plopped

next to her on the bench. "I'm done with those bumper cars. People are vicious!"

Allie suppressed a grin. "Where's your dad?"

"He's still back in there. And he's the worst," Ryan said, shaking his head. "I couldn't even turn around without him ramming into me—hard."

She patted his leg. "Look, you stay here with Cam. I need to find a restroom." She handed him her bag of cotton candy. "Don't eat it all. Save some for me." She winked at her boy.

"Thanks, Mom!"

Cam and Ryan watched her as she headed for the restroom located on the boardwalk.

Cam dug in his pocket, pulled out a roll of lifesavers. He lifted the candy to Ryan. "Want one? Or, are you too full of cotton candy?"

Ryan nodded solemnly and slid one from the roll. "No, I can manage one." He popped the candy in his mouth.

They sat in silence for several seconds before Ryan gave Cam a sidelong glance. "I found out what my dad did when we were in that store."

Cam stared into the night sky. "Maybe it's a good thing you did."

"And he borrowed my hundred dollars." He kicked his legs back and forth. "I don't think he'll pay it back."

"Yeah, maybe not." Cam cocked his head back and looked up into the darkness. "You can take after him or not, you know. It's up to you." He stared at the stars for several long seconds. "Goodness, we're sure getting a good look at the sky tonight."

Ryan thrust his arm up, pointed. "See that? That's the North Star. In the old days, before they had compasses or sextons or anything, explorers traveled the whole ocean just by following that star."

Cam popped a candy in his mouth. "Now, isn't that remarkable?"

ALLIE CAME out of her bathroom stall to find a woman leaning into the mirror, putting on lipstick.

"Well, hello, Allie." The woman put the cap back on the tube and slid it into her bag.

Allie flipped the water faucet on and drew her hands under the running water. "I'm sorry. I've met so many people since moving here. But I don't think—"

"Ellen Jeffers." The middle-aged woman extended her hand. "I run the Whale Museum located down at the Pacific Bay Lighthouse."

Allie dried her hands before taking Ellen's hand in her own. "Nice to meet you."

"Are you having fun tonight?"

"Oh, yes. Although the rides are a bit much for me."

"I see you're here with Cameron Davis."

Allie paused. "Uh-huh. We're friends," she said with caution.

Ellen looked at her warmly. "I've heard. I've also heard Cam is gaining weight lately." She studied Allie's reflection in the mirror, smiled. "You must be a good cook."

Allie grabbed a comb from her purse and straightened her hair. "Well, I'm known for being able to follow a recipe. If it's not too difficult," she quickly added.

Ellen broadened her smile. She turned and leaned her backside against the counter, folded her arms in front of her. "My daughter was friends with Cam Davis in grade school. He spent a lot of time at our house. I know him well and he sure seems cheered up lately."

Unsure how to respond, Allie tried to appear casual and returned the comb to her bag. "I can't say I've ever seen him down."

Ellen touched Allie's forearm. "Oh, honey. That man was a

wreck. He was drunk the first year. Never spoke to a soul the second." She shook her head. "He was crazy about his wife."

Allie looked long and hard at the woman before her. "Was she sick for very long? His wife?"

"Not a day in her life. She just turned around to say something to him and she dropped to the floor, dead. A brain aneurysm, they said."

Allie's breath caught, especially when she recalled her mean comment about wearing his wedding ring. "How awful," she nearly whispered.

"Oh, it was. Pure tragedy. Many of us wondered if Cam would ever be able to pick up and move on—romantically speaking." She gave Allie's arm a slight pat. "That is, until recently."

Ellen straightened, gave her a knowing look. "Well, I suppose it's time I get back. My friends are waiting. It was sure nice running into you." She moved for the door, turned, and looked back. "And I hope you'll come by the lighthouse sometime. I'd love to show you around."

The door closed behind her, leaving Allie alone. Before she could let the conversation sink in, two younger women entered the restroom, chatting.

Allie gave them a weak smile before heading for the door.

CAM LOOKED up when she slid into the bench next to him. "There you are."

"What took you so long, Mom? I thought you were just going to the bathroom." He held out what was left of her bag of cotton candy, which wasn't much. She told him to keep it, which made him smile.

"Honey, why don't you go check on your dad," she suggested.

"Sure. But I bet he won't want to leave yet."

"Well, tell him it's getting late. We should be heading home. We have to get up early in the morning."

Ryan nodded. "Okay." He ran off in the direction of the arcade.

Allie turned to Cam. "Sorry I was delayed," she said, apologizing. "I ran into one of your friends and we talked for a minute."

"Yeah, who's that?" Cam leaned over his knees and stared at out at the ocean.

"Ellen Jeffers."

"Ah," he said. "She's one of the good ones. We've known each other for years."

"Yes, that's what she said." She couldn't help but look at him differently, now that she knew his history—a story she'd never have fully guessed. Cam Davis hid his pain well.

It was then that she noticed the vacant spot where his wedding ring had been. Allie swallowed, hard.

While she wasn't prone to quick emotions, tears immediately burned at the back of her eyes. She blinked several times. "Cam," she said, his name catching in her throat. She pointed to his finger. "I—I'm so sorry. I should never have— I mean, you didn't have to—"

He covered her hand with his own, squeezed. "No. It was time."

18

Deacon Ray scooped the last bite of scrambled egg into his mouth. "What do you mean we're on our own today?"

Allie pulled the empty plate from in front of him and headed for the sink. "Just what I said. You and Ryan are going to cover things on the boat for me."

"You're not going to work? But who will skipper the boat?" He moved for his coffee mug.

Allie slipped his mug from the table and tossed the remaining coffee into the sink. "You and Ryan."

"Hey!" Deacon Ray frowned. "I was drinking that."

Allie wiped her hands on the towel, folded it, and placed it on the counter next to the sink. "Ryan!" she hollered. "Hurry. We're running late!"

Deacon Ray pushed his chair back from the table. "So, are you sick or something? You never miss work."

"Not that it's any of your business, but I'm spending the day with a friend."

"With Cam Davis." He followed her into the living room.

She pulled the wadded bedding from the sofa, started folding. "I'll drop you two off. I'm not sure when I'll be home. After you finish on the boat, you may have to get Ryan's dinner."

"But—"

"I'm asking you to step in for me today. Consider it payment for sleeping on my sofa these past weeks. Is that a problem?" She gave him a look that confirmed she wasn't teasing.

He held up his open palms in surrender. "Okay, okay. You don't have to get all riled up." He turned to Ryan, who was pulling his jacket on. "Your mom must be having her monthly girly flu."

"Watch yourself." Allie warned.

After they'd all climbed in the car, Ryan tried to break the tension. From the back seat, he leaned and put his hands on her shoulders while she was driving. "So, Mom. What *are* you doing today?"

Allie glanced in the rearview mirror. "Get your seat belt on, young man." The problem with older vehicles was they didn't have the sound alerts to warn when someone was not properly fastened in. She'd worked on her finances after everyone else had gone to bed last night, and she was definitely making progress. Even so, it'd be a while before she could entertain another car purchase.

She listened for the click. "Thanks, baby."

"You didn't answer, Mom."

Allie glanced across at the front passenger seat. Deacon Ray was thumbing through Facebook on his phone. "I'm spending the day with Mr. Davis."

Ryan grinned from the back seat. "You mean Cam?"

She sighed. "Yes, Cam."

Deacon Ray looked across the seat. "A date?"

Allie quickly shut the idea down. "No, not a date. We're—Well, he knows I'm interested in whales, and there's a museum down by the lighthouse. His good friend runs it. A woman I recently met."

Deacon Ray slipped his phone into his jacket. "Well, hey, we like whales, don't we, son? Why don't you wait, and we'll all go?"

Allie tightened her grip on the steering wheel. "We'll all go together another time." She turned on the blinker and pulled into the road leading to the marina where *Reel Time* was already loading.

Deacon Ray let out a low whistle, cocked his head and looked at her. "Don't care what you say. This kind of sounds like a date."

She pulled into a parking spot, patted her ex-husband's knee. "Like I mentioned earlier, that is none of your concern."

He put on his best pout. "Don't go getting all testy, Allie. It's just that it's our anniversary. I thought we might celebrate. As a family."

She shut off the ignition. "I don't celebrate that day anymore." Allie opened the door, glanced back at him. "By the way, our wedding anniversary was last month."

THE PACIFIC BAY lighthouse was built in the late 1800s and was located on a cliff overlooking the ocean nearly a mile north of town on a narrow point of land that jutted from the craggy shoreline. A nearby two-story keeper's dwelling now served as an interpretive center. It also housed the Whale Museum, a favorite destination for tourists and locals alike.

Cam opened the car door and Allie stepped out and into the sunshine, taking in a brightly colored mural that adorned the entire side of the building. Huge orca whales swam across the shiplap siding, through images of kelp forests, foraging for Chinook salmon.

"This is so cool," she said, smiling. "I've wanted to explore all this ever since we arrived. I just never made the time."

"A lot of people don't know that the historic Pacific Bay Lighthouse is one of eleven lighthouses located along the Oregon coast, all operated by the U.S. Coast Guard." He shut the door behind her. "All but Cape Arago are open for tours."

She surveyed the scene, shading her eyes with her hand. Looking out, the expanse of blue ocean looked beautiful and gentle, yet she knew the vast image could be deceptive. Below the cliff, waves pounded against the rocky shoreline, leaving behind a trail of angry foam.

He led her inside. Ellen Jeffers rushed out from behind her desk to greet them. "It's about time I saw your face back here." She pulled Cam into a warm embrace.

He looked a little embarrassed by her show of affection. "I believe you know my friend, Allie Barrett?"

The stack of bangle bracelets at her wrist made a clinking noise as when she waved him off. "Oh, yes. We've met."

The two women exchanged warm smiles. "Nice to see you again." Allie looped her hand through the crook in Cam's arm.

"Don't believe everything this old gal tells you," he warned. "I hear she smoked a bit too much wacky weed back in the day."

Ellen punched his arm playfully. "So not true." She gave Allie a conspiratorial look. "His father kept threatening to turn us in to law enforcement every time I pulled out a bag. Such rule followers, these two."

She jabbed a finger in his direction. "And I'm not old." She fingered the tiny bit of gray hair at her temples. "I'm *experienced*."

"Okay, I'll give you that."

"Thank you." Ellen pulled two wristbands from the top desk drawer and handed them off to Cam. "You'll need to wear these or security will run you off."

Cam grinned. "Frank still volunteers?"

She handed them each a tour brochure. "He takes his job very seriously."

Cam attached the wristband, adorned with tiny images of whales, to Allie's wrist before fastening his own. He placed his hand on Allie's back. "Ready?"

She nodded. Before they proceeded on the tour, Allie looked over her shoulder at Ellen. "Thank you," she silently mouthed.

Her new friend smiled and winked back.

The first exhibit was upstairs. The walls were colored with deep blues and greens, and painted orca whales swam all around, leaving Allie feeling like she'd entered an undersea garden.

It was fascinating to learn about how important whales were to the history of the area. The most common whale off the Oregon coast was the gray whale. In addition to the approximately two hundred resident gray whales that lived nearly year-round in the ocean waters bordering Pacific Bay, a winter and spring migration brought about tens of thousands more past the coastline.

"I've got to add whale-watching tours to *Reel Time's* schedule," she remarked. "Especially when the bottom-fishing slows."

When they'd finished looking at all the exhibits, they stopped by what looked like a vintage phone box with a sign that read *Dial-a-Whale*. By bringing the ivory-colored receiver to her ear, she could hear whale songs caught on underwater hydrophones. From the low moans and squeaks of a humpback, to the haunting call of the gray whale, and the meows and chirps of orca whales.

She loved it!

"They don't have anything like this back in Texas," she told Cam as they headed out the rear door leading to the tidal pools.

He reached and took her hand. "Well, can't say I've ever

seen a longhorn."

She laced her fingers with his, his touch causing her heart to beat fast and uneven. "You would like Texas," she told him.

They wandered down the path, hand-in-hand. "Yeah?"

"Oh, yes. Texas isn't beautiful in the same way as Oregon, I mean Oregon is lovely. But Texas has oak trees and bluebonnets and the bluest sky you've ever seen."

"Sounds amazing," he said. "Maybe I'll go sometime."

She stopped, turned. "I could take you!" The words slipped out before she thought about what she was saying. It was a bit presumptuous to suggest they'd take a trip together.

"I'd like that," he told her, putting her at ease.

It was silly how bashful she felt when he looked at her like that. Over these past weeks, their friendship had struggled to find its footing. Especially with Deacon Ray thrown in the mix. But she had to admit—she was glad they were taking it to the next step. Whatever that meant.

He must've sensed what she was thinking. "It's a little weird, isn't it? I mean, as much as I want to know you more than as just a friend, it's been a long time since I've—" He paused. "Well, since I've cared about someone."

She gave his hand a squeeze. "We can take it slow."

Cam took her by the hand and led her down the steep steps leading to the tidal waves below. "Ever touch an anemone?"

"An enemy?"

He laughed. "*An-em-o-ne*. Named after the flower for their bright colors. They're amazing, really. When you touch the center, the tiny tentacles close around your finger."

She frowned. "Does it hurt?"

"Not at all. You'll see." He pulled her farther down the path until they reached the edge of the water-slogged rocks. He pointed. "Look at the starfish."

She bent for a closer look. Her hand went to her chest. "Oh, goodness. Look how many!"

He placed his hand on her shoulder, sending a tiny shiver down her spine. She drew a deep breath, took a risk and placed her hand over the top of his.

The wind blew a strand of hair across her face. He reached up and tucked it behind her ear.

They stayed like that for nearly an hour, examining the barnacles and tiny sea creatures caught in the basins left as the tide shifted and water receded. Touching them gently, enjoying the way the light reflected off the red, yellow, and blue shells in the pools of water.

Finally, the sun lowered in the sky, signaling it was time to go.

Allie looked over at Cam. "This has been a magical day," she told him. It'd been years since she wasn't someone's daughter, someone's mother, someone's employee. Today...well, today, she no longer felt like a nun.

"You hungry?" Cam asked, offering her a hand.

"I could eat," she admitted, letting him pull her up.

"I know a great place with windows overlooking the ocean," he suggested. "And they have excellent clam chowder."

"Sounds good. Let me call and check in on Ryan first." She pulled her cell phone from her jeans pocket, dialed. Ryan picked up on the first ring. He assured her all was well. The morning's excursion had gone fine. He'd worked really hard. "Captain Paul let me steer the boat on the way home," he told her, barely able to hide his excitement.

"That's wonderful, honey. So, you and your dad are okay? You've got dinner covered? There's leftover enchiladas in the fridge," she reminded.

Over the years, she'd rarely left Ryan alone with his father. It wasn't that she didn't trust Deacon Ray...oh, who was she kidding? She didn't trust Deacon Ray. She did, however, trust Ryan.

"I'll put some in the microwave," he assured her. "We're

going to watch re-runs on television."

She started to ask what programs when he intercepted her interrogation. "Only good shows, Mom. I promise." She smiled to herself.

Allie ended the call and slipped her phone back in her pocket. "Looks like everything's fine at home."

Cam nodded, pleased. "Good. I wasn't ready to end our time together."

The restaurant was just as he'd promised. Perched on a cliff, the Bay House offered three-hundred-sixty-degree magnificent views through banks of windows overlooking the ocean. They were greeted, then seated at a table next to a fireplace with crackling flames. Even late-summer evenings could stir up a chill, and the fire was a welcome touch.

"I hope you love seafood," Cam said, looking over his menu.

They ordered manila clams in drawn butter sauce, crab cakes and chinook salmon covered with white-wine hollandaise sauce. For dessert, they enjoyed crème brûlée with a crust of hard caramelized sugar and a cup of coffee laced with a heavy dose of Bailey's Irish Cream liqueur.

When she could eat no more, she leaned back in her chair, raised her open hands. "I give. That was wonderful, but I can't wedge one more thing into my stomach."

Cam lifted his coffee for a final sip. "Sounds like we need a walk on the beach."

He paid the bill, and they made their way outside and down a narrow set of stairs leading to the sand. The sun descended on the horizon, leaving a hint of orange at the skyline.

Allie pulled her jacket closer against the breeze, which prompted Cam to place his arm around her shoulders. It felt good, the way he casually let his arm drape. It was as if they were old pros at this dating stuff.

Up ahead, a white-haired woman leaned her head against a man's shoulder as they made their way along the shoreline.

"Will you look at that?" Cam said, motioning toward the frail couple.

She and Cam slowed their pace, watching them intently until eventually, the aged couple stopped, and the woman bent to pick up a shell.

"Tell me about your wife." As soon as the words were out of her mouth, Allie felt a case of nerves. What made her think Cam would want to talk about his dead wife—the loss that had nearly taken him under?

Too often, she spoke before she thought. Her mama had often said just that. And it was true. Case in point was the pained look that immediately sprouted on Cam's face.

"What do you want to know?"

Allie immediately grew apologetic. She'd crossed the line. "You don't have to tell me. I shouldn't have asked."

He stopped, turned to face her. "What do you want to know?"

Slightly ashamed at her bold intrusion, she gave him a weak smile, searched for a safe way to start. "How did you meet?" Her heart thudded as she waited for him to respond.

He scanned the sunset as if the answer was in the fading sun. "Thank you," he said, squeezing her hand.

"Huh?" Allie grew confused. "What do you mean?"

"I mean, no one ever asks me about Julia. She's gone, but at times it feels as if people want to act as though she never existed." He grew wistful. "I know they think talking about her hurts. It's just the opposite."

They started walking, the moist sand underfoot giving way a little with each step.

"You must have loved her very much."

He nodded. "Yes, but even more, we were best friends."

Allie understood. Despite immense difficulties, her own parents remained soul mates—so committed to one another, nothing could pull them apart. Not even her daddy's struggles with alcohol could wedge their hearts apart. She could argue her mama's life may have been much easier if she'd moved on. That was never an option. A deep love bound them together.

Sadly, that had not been her own marital experience.

"Julia and I met at school. I was in my final year at Oregon State, and she was a freshman. She'd just come out of the MU, that was the name of our student union building. I remember how her long hair swung slightly as she clipped down the front steps, her arms loaded with textbooks. She was trying to juggle those heavy volumes while checking a campus map—with little success." He grinned. "Sounds a bit cliché, but I offered to carry her books."

"Not at all. Sounds...thoughtful."

Cam shrugged. "I don't know about that. All I remember is how the moment I saw her, I wanted to meet her."

"How long before you married?"

For some reason, my question struck Cam as funny. He let out a big infectious laugh. "Julia wasn't known for making quick decisions about anything. She'd ponder for ten minutes whether to add creamer to her coffee—every morning. And I learned never to walk down the cereal aisle with her in the grocery store. She'd turn every box and read the nutritional values carefully. In the end, she always bought her favorite Cocoa Pebbles, stating there were some things worth the sugar content."

Cam placed his arm around Allie. "Likewise, I might not have been her best choice. She had plans—big plans. Wanted to be a political journalist, head off to New York or Washington, D.C. Marrying me meant giving up on that dream. No matter my urging to consider her future, she couldn't seem to put me back on the shelf."

In the distance, someone whistled at their barking dog.

"We were married nearly seventeen years before I ever brought the subject up again," he continued. "When I mentioned it, she quickly shut down the notion saying living with me had been the adventure of a lifetime. Four hours later..." Cam paused. "Well, she was dead."

"That must've been so hard—losing her so suddenly."

"Men deal with losing a spouse differently. We get angry—or at least I did. I was in a private rage for months. Didn't even attempt to talk to anyone about the absolute void my life had become. Did all kinds of destructive things." Cam shook his head. "It was a reckless way to live.'

"In the end, I knew Julia wouldn't want me to remain all maudlin. She'd want me to live well. So, I honor her by trying every day to do just that." He looked at her then. "What about you? While different, you suffered loss as well."

His insight left her feeling warm inside. "Yes, I suppose you're right. While I didn't lose my spouse to death, my feelings for him certainly died a little every time I caught him with someone else."

Allie focused on the dimmed horizon, deciding to be brave. She needed to be as transparent as Cam had been. "I'd probably wondered before, 'If my husband cheated on me, what would I do?' Throw him out? Bankrupt him? Never let him see our Ryan again? Sure, that's what we women in that situation think we would do. But that's all just hypothetical.

"Rare is the woman who says, 'If my husband cheated on me, I'd take him back.' Of course not. Who stays with a cheater? Well, statistically, a lot of women do—most, in fact, including me. Yes, I'm one of the eighty-one percent of women who stayed with their husbands after they were unfaithful. At least that's what the internet statistics revealed.

"But let me tell you something: I was just as surprised that I stayed as anyone."

She swallowed hard before continuing. "I'd had my doubts about the amount of time Deacon Ray was spending with a female coworker down at the tire shop where he worked at the time. But the store had just been acquired by a big corporation in Dallas with a big project. There was a team of people sent to help with the transition. Deacon Ray told me he'd been assigned to help the team. So, when he started staying late, it made sense—or so I told myself. Besides, this was the first time I'd seen him take that much initiative. Then I saw texts from that woman on his phone that didn't seem work-related.'

"Then, one night, when he was away on a business trip. Now mind you, Deacon Ray had never gone a business trip in his entire life. Still, I thought I needed to believe him.'

"Anyway, one night I tried to reach him and I couldn't. Suddenly, I just knew. There's no other way to describe it. I tried to convince myself that I was being paranoid. I tried to tell myself the woman I suspected wasn't even that pretty.'

"My friends agreed. 'With her?' they scoffed when I shared my niggling concern. 'Don't be ridiculous.'"

"The next day, when he finally answered his phone, I demanded the truth. And he gave it to me—partly. They kissed once. Well, more than once, he quickly reneged.

"I insisted he come home immediately if he had even the tiniest bit of hope of salvaging our marriage. He did. While he drove the few hours back, I walked around our house wringing my shaking hands like Lady Macbeth. I was in shock. What was I going to do?" I moaned out loud.'

"Over the next few days, the full story eventually trickled out. My husband confessed that he had been having on-again, off-again affairs for years. Yes—multiple times.

"Like so many who discover a partner's betrayal, my emotions were all over the place. I would shake my husband awake at three a.m., demanding to know 'Why? Why did you do it? Weren't we happy?'

Allie paused, took a deep breath. "My fury shook the house. 'How dare he?' I would fume. 'What was wrong with him?' I'd vacillate between rage and exhaustion. Every day, I was trying to be the best mom I could, while also trying to go to my own job every day. So, I just kept putting one foot in front of the other. Later, I figured. Later, I'd decide whether to stay or go."

Allie stared over at Cam. "Because here's what no one tells you about infidelity: It's so bring-you-to-your-knees devastating that kicking him out is the last thing you have the energy to do. It takes everything you've got to just breathe, to stem the bleeding, to tuck your kid into bed at night without curling up beside them weeping."

She sighed. "But I couldn't let Ryan see me like that. He was far too young at that time to understand why his mom was falling apart. And I'm not the sort to lie to my kid. I figured he might find out eventually, though I couldn't imagine telling them the whole story. Not then, and not even now. But deciding to kick Deacon Ray out? Maybe later, I thought. But right then? Right then, I just needed to figure out how to get dressed for work, and make lunch for Ryan, and cancel the dentist appointment that I couldn't imagine going to with an affair-sized boulder in my gut."

"I wanted to fight for my marriage," she said. "But frankly, I didn't have the energy. I felt like I was fighting for my life. I lost weight, enough that people who'd previously said I looked 'great' began to ask if I was okay. I didn't tell them what was going on. I couldn't bear the pity or the scorn." She picked at some lint on her pants.

"That's another part of cheating that we don't talk about enough. Often times, people assume that if a man cheats, that means his wife was a witch, a nag. She let herself go. The other woman was sexy and interesting. He was trading up. Which is why it's so shocking to so many of us that our husbands cheated with someone who looked, well, ordinary."

Allie lifted her chin. "Because here's yet another thing nobody tells you about infidelity: Deacon Ray didn't cheat because there was something wrong with me, or even our marriage. He cheated because there was something wrong with him. Like every other aspect of Deacon Ray's life, he thought he could find the answer in a fantasy."

"I went to a therapist," she continued. "I was urged me to give myself as long as I needed to sort this out, and to learn to trust myself. Trust myself? I'd somehow missed the fact that my husband was having multiple affairs, that he was irresponsible and I was carrying the entire weight of the relationship. How could I ever trust myself?'

A sad smile lifted the corners of her lips. "Finally, it dawned on me that I shouldn't be the only one working to save our marriage, that Deacon Ray would continue this behavior, and I couldn't—" Allie felt a slight chill, even though Cam's arm tightened around her shoulders. "That's when I found him again. With a different girl."

Allie's throat tightened. "Believe me, living with someone who can't love you back? Way lonelier than actually being alone." She paused. "I didn't have the energy to be mad anymore. I simply took off my wedding ring."

Allie swallowed. She had never opened her heart and poured out her story to another human being. She suspected, neither had he.

They shared, it seemed, an uncommon intimacy. Not based on the length of time they'd known each other, but some sort of instant recognition on an unconscious level. Something told her that their souls somehow knew each other.

When he took her home that night, Cam walked her across her front deck. He turned to face her, sandwiching himself close as she neared the door.

"I—I'll see you tomorrow?" she whispered, reaching for the knob while never breaking gaze.

Something inside compelled him to pull her close. Never would she forget the look—his eyes filled with yearning as he dragged her to him.

Despite the longing she too felt inside, she tensed.

"I can stop," he offered, in a choked voice.

Near breathless, she leaned into him. "Please don't. I'm tired of being anti-social."

Cam pulled her tighter. She could feel the rise and fall of his chest, the hot press of his arm at the small of her back, the wild hammering of her own pulse in her ears. All at once, she was painfully aware of his nearness, bare inches away from the dark stubble that peppered his jaw. His breathing was ragged like hers, warm and sweet as his gaze lowered to her lips.

He kissed her full on the mouth, and heat shivered through her. Their souls were not the only connection, her body wanted him as well.

Somewhere deep inside, beneath the passion he stirred, she could see things clearly. She wanted to love again—to experience the full measure of a relationship, and she wanted it with him.

When Cam finally pulled back, his face was flush with a wide grin. "Meeting you was fate, becoming your friend was a choice, but this? Well, what's happening now feels—"

"Feels happily out of control," she finished.

They shared a laugh, promised to talk tomorrow.

Inside, she slowly closed the door and leaned against it, grinning. If a date could be perfect—that one certainly was very close.

Across the room, the television blared some old episode of *Baywatch*. Allie grabbed the remote and clicked it off.

Deacon Ray reclined on the sofa, his head tucked back against the cushion, his eyes shut and mouth wide open. Every breath he exhaled sounded like a high-pitched coffee grinder. Next to him, Ryan lay wedged against his chest, a sweet smile of contentment on his face. He was sound asleep as well.

Allie sighed and covered them with a blanket, then headed for bed.

19

"So—you were out late. Where'd the two of you go?" Deacon Ray glanced across the table. "Is that a blueberry muffin?"

Allie nodded, shoved the plate of muffins closer to him. "What I do on my dates are none of your business."

Her ex grabbed a muffin and slathered butter across the top. "Oh, now, don't go get all testy. I was only trying to be polite —be interested in, you know, your life."

She gave him a skeptical look. "Right." She turned to Ryan. "Baby, I'm going to need you to get dressed quickly this morning. I want to get down to the docks early. We have a large group going out this morning for our first whale-watching excursion. It's going to be exciting." She turned to Deacon Ray. "By the way, I could use your help."

"Would love to," he told her. "But I'm already committed. I met a guy who needs some work done on his bike. I told him I'd help him out. He lives in Seaside, and he just texted he's on his way."

Allie held back an eye-roll. "Well, I hope you're getting paid." She made a point of directing her attention to the muffin he crammed in his mouth. "The grocery bill around here is getting a bit out-of-hand."

"That reminds me. Did you pick me up a bag of pistachios? And I'm out of deodorant."

She groaned inside. "You didn't answer my question."

"Oh, getting paid? No, we agreed to swap," he said, still chewing. "The guy's giving me a pair of saddlebags that are too big for his new bike."

Allie glanced over at Ryan, who was watching their exchange with interest. "Well then, perhaps you can help out and do the dishes. And start dinner. I have a chicken you can put in the Crock-Pot."

"The Crock-Pot?"

"Yeah, that's the thing you can plug in and it cooks for you all day," Ryan quickly explained. "Even I can use it. And I'm a kid."

Allie pushed herself from the table, stood. "Okay, no more chit-chat. Finish up, Ryan. Let's go."

Minutes later, they were in the car and on their way. The early light of the day filtered in through the car windows. Last night's forecast for rain had fizzled. Instead, the late summer morning sky was unblemished and the sun sparkled as it peeked over the horizon.

Ryan looked across the seat at her as she reached and turned the radio on. "So, where *did* you go last night, Mom?" He had a dab of jam at the corner of his mouth.

Allie pulled to the stoplight, wet her finger and rubbed the jam away. "I told you. I spent the evening with Cameron Davis." The radio crackled. She banged the dashboard twice for good measure. When she did, the sound cleared.

Ryan picked at his jeans. "A date?"

Her brows pulled together in a puzzled frown. "Well, kind of. We went to the Whale Museum, and then we caught a bite to eat."

Ryan cocked his head, stared at her. "Does that mean you and Dad aren't—I mean, he lives with us again. I thought maybe you and he would be together."

She immediately shook her head. "No, honey. We're divorced. I'm letting him stay temporarily. That's all."

"But Dad said—"

Allie scowled. "What did your Dad say?"

Ryan shifted in the seat. "Well, he said that you were destined to be together. He said families should stay together."

Anger boiled inside her. "Oh, he did, did he?" Allie fought to keep from pounding the steering wheel with her fist. Did he also say dads should tell the truth? That dads shouldn't borrow money from their kids and not pay it back? Did he tell Ryan daddies shouldn't have girlfriends?

"*We* are not a family. Your dad and I are most certainly not a couple. He's your father. That's all."

The minute the hot, angry words spewed from her mouth, she was sorry. Especially when she saw the wounded look on her son's face, leaving little doubt the verbal eruption had bruised his soul.

"I'm sorry," she quickly offered. "Baby, I—"

Behind them, a car honked. Allie looked up to find the light had turned green. She glared in the rearview mirror. "All right, all right!" She quickly pulled forward, then maneuvered the car to the side of the road and put the old Blazer in park.

"Look, son." She twisted to face Ryan. She rubbed his arm with affection. "Your dad will always be special to me because he gave me you, but we won't be getting married to each other again."

Ryan pulled his arm away. "But, Mom—"

Allie shook her head. "No buts, sweetheart. We don't love each other like that."

Ryan teared up. "But that's not what Dad said. He says he still loves you. He always has. He wants us to be a family again."

Allie gritted her teeth. How dare Deacon Ray misuse her son's emotions. "He may want that, and he will always be your dad. But he isn't my husband anymore." *For very good reason,* she refrained from adding.

She drew a deep breath, kicking herself for trusting Deacon Ray. She'd made a mistake letting her ex-husband stay on and weasel into their lives. She also should have had a heart-to-heart with Ryan before ever taking a step toward a new relationship.

She could build a ladder to the moon with all her missteps.

The worst? She could just kick herself for not realizing the impact all this might have on her son. She assumed he'd adjusted, that he was aware that things were forever over between her and Deacon Ray. She'd forgotten how much he yearned for a family, and for what she too had been so reluctant to let go of for so long—*the dream.*

How could she have forgotten he was only a kid, a lonely boy who desperately wanted a father in his life? Because of that, he was willing to overlook all the ways Deacon Ray had failed him.

She couldn't.

Especially since very little evidence existed to show he'd embraced any sort of sorrow for what he'd done, or any change in his behavior. She knew it would be just a matter of time before some gal half his age (and double her own bra size) would be hanging off his arm.

Deacon Ray was still Deacon Ray.

She'd had to face that back when she sat across the desk from that divorce attorney and signed the papers that would start the process of ending a relationship that had hurt her—and Ryan. As much as she'd wanted things to be different, they simply weren't.

It was time she squared up with that truth yet again.

"Honey." She squeezed Ryan's knee. "Your dad is a good

man in a lot of ways. But he's—well, he also makes very bad decisions. Decisions that hurt the ones he loves sometimes."

Her son shook his head. "But he's trying to change, Mom. He said so. We just need to give him a chance."

This time she teared up. How could she make her sweet boy understand?

Allie patted his leg, touched the soft skin along his jaw. He would be a man soon, but not yet. Today, he was still a boy. "Look, the important thing is that both of us love you very much. That will never change, no matter what. Despite the fact your parents are no longer married, you still have both of us in your corner, and we both are here for you." Despite the promise she'd just made, she wondered just how long Deacon Ray would hang around once she cut off his meal ticket.

No—she knew the answer. There was little doubt he would fail to hold down a job and become responsible. She'd have to face the inevitability that her ex-husband was bound to move on when she asked him to leave the house. She'd simply have to try to explain to Ryan when the time came to cut him off.

And the time was coming—sooner than later.

20

Allie liked to greet their passengers before they boarded, but this morning her unanticipated talk with Ryan had delayed her opportunity to welcome today's patrons until after they'd ascended the loading ramp and were walking the deck of *Reel Time*.

After a wave at Captain Paul, she quickly hung up her outer jacket in the tiny closet located inside the cabin, then grabbed the microphone and turned the public address system on. "Hello, everyone. I'm Allie Barrett, and this is my son, Ryan. We're the owners of this vessel." She loved how Ryan's face beamed whenever she included him in that introduction. He needed that lift this morning. "Welcome aboard! Captain Paul will be guiding us out this morning. He's already let me know that he's hearing chatter from other boats that there have been numerous whale sightings this morning."

Allie donned her brightest voice, recited the spiel she'd memorized. "Today, we'll be following the sea wall until we hit open waters. Our excursion will take us approximately five to ten miles offshore. Each year, thousands of these magnificent creatures migrate south from their feeding grounds in the

Bering Sea while heading to their breeding grounds in Baja, Mexico. These warm-water lagoons become nurseries for expectant mothers. Then in the spring, the whales migrate north back to Alaska. You'll want to watch closely today for two whale behaviors—spy hopping, where the head sticks straight up out of the water—and breaching, where a half to three-quarters of the body length comes out of the water and falls on its side or back causing a tremendous splash."

The excitement of the tourists was evident in their excited chatter as they laid claim to their spots along the railing. Many had binoculars hanging from their necks. Others carried expensive cameras, hoping to catch the perfect shot.

Allie quickly looked around for Ryan. She spotted him among the crowd with a couple of kids his age. He'd studied up on everything he could about whales and was generously sharing additional information. "Gray whales are about the length of a school bus," he explained to his new friends, sounding just like the guy he'd watched on YouTube. "And their weight equals about ten elephants each." The kids were impressed with his knowledge, particularly a little girl with braids. They all linked arms, and Ryan pulled his new friends to the bow of the boat, the prime watching spot.

Allie smiled. It appeared Ryan had put the matter of his father aside. At least for the time being. Like all children from broken homes, her son had been through a lot. She'd done her best to shelter him and make him feel secure. Thankfully, he was resilient.

That did not mean she wouldn't have to address the situation with Deacon Ray, and soon. Until then, she'd focus on the things at hand. Practice some of that resiliency herself and not dwell on the negative aspects of life. Like her mama always said, "Despite what troubles may come, life had a way of ending up better than you ever expected."

The excursion ended up being an extremely profitable one,

in terms of whale sightings. At last count, by the time the boat pulled back into dock, eighteen sightings were reported. All in all, a great day.

Allie waved and bid goodbye to all their passengers as they disembarked, thanking them for choosing *Reel Time*. She grinned as one silver-haired woman drew her into a hug. "Seeing the impressive whale spout and then that enormous tail slap the water was an experience that was on my bucket list. I can go home to the Lord a very happy woman." The woman tucked a twenty-dollar tip into Allie's palm. "Thank you so very much."

Allie gave the tourists a final wave before anxiously pulling her phone from her pocket. Cell service was often spotty until the boat returned closer to the shoreline. Now that they were back, she wanted to see if she had a text from Cam.

He didn't disappoint.

Enjoyed last night very much. We need a re-do soon. I'll call you.

Allie read his text. Try as she might, she couldn't help but smile. She tucked the phone back in her pants pocket, feeling slightly giddy. Despite the perplexities they both faced in leaving the old behind and moving on into a new relationship, the effort held a lot of promise.

Her heart sped up just thinking about him.

Cameron Davis looked handsome in a way that suggested he didn't realize just how handsome he was. There was no effort involved. No self-awareness. He was tall and lean with broad shoulders and strong arms. His jawline was strong and angled, his hair warm brown. A gray undertone peeked from green eyes. She loved the way those eyes looked at her.

A colony of seagulls screeched overhead as they dove to meet a bucket of fish entrails tossed into the water by a man wearing bright-yellow rubber overalls.

"Mom, wait for me!" Ryan called out as he scurried down the gangplank toward her.

As he drew near, she ruffled his hair. "What? You think I'd leave you?"

He grinned. "Did you see all my new friends?"

"I did. Looked like you were having fun today." She led him to the car, motioned for him to get in. "What was her name?"

He blushed ever so slightly. "Who?"

"The cutie with the braids. What was her name?" She moved to the driver's side and got in, shoved the keys in the ignition.

He shrugged. "Beth, I think."

"Does she live close?"

"Nah, her family lives in Michigan. Her mom and dad, and her little brother. I haven't checked a map yet, but I think that's pretty far away."

She could see disappointment on his face and decided to change the subject. "Remember, we're having chicken and noodles tonight. You love chicken and noodles."

"Mom?" he said, looking over at her.

"Yeah, bud?"

"So, you're sure you're never going to marry Dad again?"

Once again, the question broadsided her. She thought she'd cleared up the subject. Obviously, the issue still plagued his mind. "Honey, we talked about that this morning, remember?"

"Yeah, but if you don't love Dad anymore, do you think he'll leave?"

21

When they arrived home, Deacon Ray was out front working on his bike.

"We need to talk," she told him. She sent Ryan inside. "Honey, wash up and set the table."

Deacon Ray stood, ran his hand through his hair. "Uh, I kind of forgot to put the chicken in the Crock-Pot this morning." He looked sheepish. "And uh, the chicken had to be tossed. Left it out on the counter."

Allie stared at the stains on his T-shirt, contemplated how badly she'd love to land a punch right above the larger spot. Instead, she took a deep breath and forced a calm she didn't feel inside. "Fine. We'll have sloppy joes." She called to Ryan, who seemed to have slowed his pace on the way to the front door. "Get some hamburger out of the freezer and put it in the microwave to thaw. Don't forget to put a pie plate underneath."

Deacon Ray brightened. He pointed at his bike. "So, what do you think?"

"Think?"

"Of the new saddlebags," he told her. "Ain't they a beauty? A pair like those would cost a couple of hundred at the Harley store. I don't think the guy even knew the value of what he had." He seemed to take great pleasure in the fact.

"Deacon Ray, we need to talk," she repeated, this time with her hands parked on her hips.

Her ex-husband wiped his hands on his handkerchief, stuffed it back in his rear pocket. "What's up," he said, donning an innocent look. "I mean, if this is about the chicken, I'll buy us another."

Ryan's face appeared in the living room window, pressed against the glass.

"It's not about the chicken." She took Deacon Ray's arm, led him several steps down the path, just to be sure they would not be overheard by their son. "Look. Apparently, you've been putting some misguided ideas in Ryan's head. Ideas about us getting back together."

Deacon Ray's open palms flew up. "Now, Allie. I—"

"Save it!" She suddenly felt overheated, despite the slight ocean breeze brushing against her bare arms. "Look, Deacon Ray. We need some boundaries. First, the subject of you and me —" She made a circling motion with her finger. "Well, anything about you and me is off-limits. That includes discussions with our son, or anyone else. Second, the subject of me and Cam is completely off-limits. My love life is just that—mine. It is not yours to ponder, or to share with anyone else. Got it? Third, you can't stay here. For Ryan's sake, I'm not sending you packing tonight. But it's time we develop an exit strategy. And, soon."

Deacon Ray reached for her. She pulled back. "No," she told him. "None of this is negotiable."

He grinned. "I got a job."

She stared at him, confused. "What do you mean you got a job?"

"Just that," he said. "I heard what you said this morning. I need to pull my weight. So, I went and got duly employed."

The revelation shocked her. "Well, that is news." Welcome

news, she might add. The fact Deacon Ray had secured a job was certainly a step in the right direction. Perhaps he would stick around for Ryan after all.

She had mixed feelings about him remaining near, of course. She'd certainly prefer for him to get on that fancy new bike and head on down the road, as far away as possible. But for her son's sake, the fact Deacon Ray had a job was a welcome development, a great first step.

As if reading her next thought, Deacon Ray quickly added, "And I'll be getting my own place too. As soon as I get my first paycheck." He rubbed the back of his neck. "I appreciate you letting me stay on and all." He looked back toward the house, where Ryan's face remained plastered against the window. "He's my kid, you know?"

Guilt flooded Allie.

Perhaps she'd miscalculated the situation. What if people like Deacon Ray could change after all?

"Deacon Ray, I'd never stand in the way of you and Ryan. You know that. In fact, I'm glad you plan to stay around, that you want to be a full-time father to him. He needs you." She smiled and turned to go into the house, then paused and turned. "Deacon Ray, you didn't say where you were going to go to work?"

Deacon Ray wiped a spot off the chrome on his bike, shoved the hanky back in his pocket. "I'm the new deckhand for Anthony Charters."

22

"You think I should be worried?" Cam pulled open the door to the Pig 'n' Pancake. "About Deacon Ray going to work for Craig Anthony?" He paused, waited for her to enter, then followed her inside. "Let me put it this way, Craig Anthony never makes a move without a well-planned strategy to benefit him, and him alone. From what you tell me, your ex-husband's employment history isn't exactly stellar. So, what does Craig gain by hiring Deacon Ray?"

The smell of hamburgers frying hit her nostrils and made her stomach growl. "I have to admit, I wondered that as well."

Muncy hurried over from behind the counter to greet them, wiping his hands on a towel tucked into his apron. "Well, there you two are! I've got your food ready to go. Over here." Cam's dad motioned to the end of the counter, where a large sack bulging with their picnic lunch waited. "I packed up some loaves of sourdough bread and some cheese. Oh, and a nice bottle of pinot noir." He grinned and handed Cam the bag. "Should go really nice with those oysters."

"Thanks, Dad." Cam took the bag and pulled his father into a one-armed hug. "I appreciate it."

Muncy waved him off. "No problem. Hope you two have fun." He winked at them. Clearly, Cam's dad was happy they were seeing one another romantically.

Outside, Cam led her to where they'd leaned their bikes against a white picket fence lined with hydrangea bushes. She ran her fingers across a fat purple bloom, appreciating its beauty.

After learning this Texas girl had never eaten oysters, Cam talked her into going on a bike ride to the Pacific Bay Oyster Farm—an eight-mile trip down a winding road that circled the bay.

The plan was to enjoy a picnic and sample some of the prized shellfish grown in the brackish backwaters of an inlet lined with tall Douglas firs. Despite her initial reluctance ("They look gross," she told him) he cajoled her by saying the owners had the best smoked oysters around. "Keep an open mind. I promise you won't be sorry."

The morning was glorious, a day you might see in a magazine or marketing brochure, sunny and warm without a cloud in the sky—the kind of fall weather that lured tourists into longing to make the Oregon coast their home.

"Thank you so much for doing this with me." Cam secured their lunch items inside the basket on her bike. "It's going to be great. I just want you to know that if we have to stop and rest along the way, it's completely fine. No pressure, okay?"

"Oh, so you think I'm a physical wimp?" She teased him with a broad smile and took hold of the handlebars, walked her bike to the edge of the road.

"Now, I didn't say that. I only wanted you to know that if you get tired and—"

Allie waved him off, lifted her chin. "You just worry about you, mister."

Cam led the way because he knew the route. Allie followed along, memorizing his back and his T-shirt and the speed at which he moved his legs. The day was fun, though about four miles in, the ride started to get a little boring. Despite the gorgeous scenery, the soaring pines and the fern-lined roadway—the bay in the distance filled with boat masts jutting toward the sky—they couldn't talk much. Allie decided to sing some songs in her head until she noticed Cam pointing ahead. "We're here," he shouted over his shoulder.

He pulled into a drive made of tiny white shells and immediately hopped off his bike, unable to peddle any further on the rough surface. "You ready to eat?" he asked, pointing to a picnic table.

She dismounted her bike. "You bet. I'm starving."

They removed their helmets and biking gloves, then rinsed their hands at a faucet on the side of the building.

"We made good time," he said. "Didn't even have to stop and take a break."

A smile slowly crossed Allie's face. "You're like a dog with a bone," she teased. "My legs feel it though. It's been a while since I've biked that far."

"Goodness, this is amazing," she remarked, taking in the picturesque vista. Large structures with conveyors and pulleys lined the shoreline of the inlet. Beyond, wooden piers woven with boardwalks with wooden slats spaced several feet apart stretched into the brackish water.

A large wooden sign posted at the entrance read "Pacific Bay Oysters – Founded 1907."

The store itself was rather nondescript, a wooden building painted white with no architectural features to speak of. At either side of the entrance, metal benches painted green lined the doorway. A large pot of pink petunias with flowing blue lobelia was the only indication the building was a retail outlet and not another processing structure.

"Ready?" Cam asked, pointing to the door.

Allie nodded and followed him inside where she was surprised to find the interior commercial looking. Linoleum similar to the flooring in her mama's old kitchen stretched across the small space to a glass-cased counter. Inside the counter were a variety of Cryovac bags filled with smoked oysters. In addition to the regular variety, some were hickory smoked, some barbeque flavored, and some were flavored with garlic. A large metal cooler with three glass doors lined the wall. Inside were large netted bags filled with oysters in the shell.

"Interesting," she whispered in Cam's direction, her nose scrunched.

"Don't mind the smell," he cautioned. "You are in for a treat."

A woman, who looked to be in her sixties, appeared from a back room. Her glasses were tucked up in her blonde hair, and she wore bright red lipstick and a white apron. "Hey, Cameron. What can I get you for?"

Cam stepped forward. "Hey, Grace. How are you?"

The woman wiped her hands on a towel. "Good. Real Good. You?"

"Couldn't be better. And Wylie?"

"That ole hoot got a wild wind and took the boys up to Alaska for a fishing trip."

"A vacation?" Cam looked utterly surprised.

She nodded. "Oh, yeah. I was as surprised as you. I don't think Wylie's been more than a two-hour drive from this place in the last five years." She looked at Allie. "He was born just down the road and claims this place is his lifeblood."

She glanced back at Cam. "And who's your pretty friend?"

Cam grinned. "This is Allie Barrett. Her and her boy moved here recently."

"Oh, you're that girl from Texas I heard about. Tarver McIntosh's niece."

Allie reached out a hand. "Yes, I live in his old place."

Grace shook her head. "Well, you certainly had your hands full fixing that place up. I hear you are doing right okay though. Surprised all those boys down at the brewery," she looked at Cam. "You know how those boys like to talk."

She pulled her glasses down onto her nose. "And I hear your ex-husband showed up unannounced."

Allie shifted on her feet uncomfortably, disdaining the fact her situation had been discussed by the townspeople. No doubt they wondered why she hadn't sent him packing already. Frankly, she had wondered the same thing.

Grace shook her head. "Men." As if that one word said it all. She quickly added, "This one here? Well, he's one of the good ones."

"Thanks, Grace. Coming from you, that's high praise."

"You here for some oysters?" she asked.

When Cam confirmed that they were, she pointed to the wall. "The prices are all up there on the whiteboard. The morning pull looked really good. Our Kumomotos are small, but oh, they are delicious. Nutty and sweet."

Cam pulled his billfold from his back pocket. "Sounds good. Shuck us each a dozen. We'll take two bags of each of the smoked oysters as well."

"Do you need some lemons and Tabasco?"

"Absolutely!" He leaned over the counter in a conspiratorial manner. "You don't happen to have the fryer going in the back?"

Grace beamed. "Well, only for our favorite customers. You want a few battered up?"

"Allie's never tasted an oyster. I want her to have the full experience."

With oysters in hand, they made their way outside to a grassy area with picnic tables overlooking the inlet.

Cam unwrapped the bread and cheese. He handed her a paper plate loaded with their lunchtime treats. "Here you go. Enjoy!"

Allie lifted her eyebrows. She wasn't exactly filled with an adventurous spirit when it came to trying odd foods. She didn't care what anyone said, a slimy glob in a shell didn't seem palatable.

She stared long and hard across the table at Cameron. A smile slowly crossed his face. "What's the matter?" he asked.

"You—you're going to eat it raw?"

"Yup. They're good battered and fried and smoked. But right out of the half-shell is my favorite."

"Go ahead, try it. Here, let me show you." He squeezed a liberal amount of lemon over the meat in his half shell, then dribbled Tabasco over the top. Finished, he lifted the oyster to his mouth, tipped it back into his mouth.

His eyes closed as if he were having an out-of-body experience or something.

When he finally looked at her, she couldn't help but grin.

"What?" he asked. "I like oysters."

"Clearly." She tenuously pulled the plate toward her, mimicked Cam by squeezing lemon and Tabasco sauce over her so-called treat. Pulling her eyes closed, the same way she did just before she got an immunization injection, she quickly lifted the shell to her lips and tipped.

Her taste buds were immediately hit with a sharp saltiness followed by an almost sweet, nutty flavor. The texture was soft —almost buttery.

Her eyes widened. "You're right," she exclaimed with surprise. "They are good."

"Told you." He dug in the bag and pulled out a disposable plastic container. "Looks like Dad sent along some of his famous macaroni salad."

She took a big bite that left a smidge of mayonnaise on the

side of her mouth. She wanted to laugh at herself, but her mouth was too full.

Cam took one of the napkins from the bag, reached out and gently wiped the side of her mouth.

"Thanks," she said, swallowing both the food and her pride.

"I don't know how to thank you," she said softly. Her heart filled with a rush of emotion. "I was hoping for a lot of things when I packed my car with my son and drove all the way to Oregon. I longed for a home of my own, sufficient income, a good community in which to raise Ryan. I never expected to find such a good friend."

Cam didn't answer; it wasn't necessary. He simply reached across the picnic table, took her hand and squeezed.

23

When Allie returned home from her bike ride with Cam, she tossed her jacket over the back of her armchair, wondering why the room was so quiet. Normally, she'd come home to find Deacon Ray and Ryan on the sofa playing video games or watching television.

"Ryan?" she called out.

Her son appeared from down the hall with a book in hand. "Hey, Mom. What's up?"

"I was going to ask you the same thing. Where's your dad?"

Ryan shrugged. "He got a text from that guy who gave him the saddlebags for his bike. Said he had to go meet up with him, and he'd be home later."

Allie drew Ryan into a brief hug, kissed the top of his head. "What time was that?"

"Just after lunch," he answered. Seeing the look on her face, he quickly lifted his book. "But it's okay. I'm reading this really good book. It's called *The Lion, the Witch and the Wardrobe*. I got it at the library. You see, there's these kids who enter another world from this closet and—"

She smiled at him. "I've read it, sweetheart."

"Then you know all about Narnia and the evil white witch."

She ruffled his hair. "Loved the story."

The door opened, and Deacon Ray walked in carrying a pizza box. "Hey, y'all," he said, making his way to the kitchen. "I bought dinner."

"Where's your bike, Dad?"

"My bike?" He hiccoughed. "Well, your ole dad had a few beers with the boys down at the bike shop." He looked at Allie. "I was a good boy and didn't drive home."

"Thank goodness for small favors," she muttered.

"Oh, now, don't go getting your panties in a wad, Allie." He held up the box like a prize before tossing it on the table. "I bought Canadian Bacon and pineapple, just like you like." Ignoring her dirty look, he leaned to his son. "A girlie pizza."

There was no doubt in her mind, her ex-husband had consumed more than a few beers. She didn't like that kind of influence around Ryan. "Ryan, honey—could you give your dad and me a few minutes?"

Ryan immediately grew concerned. "But the pizza."

"Please." Allie gave him a look. Her request was not negotiable.

Deacon Ray let out a nervous laugh before he stumbled, caught himself. "Go on, son. I think I'm in trouble with your ma." He winked, which only served to make her more upset.

She listened for Ryan's bedroom door to close. "Now, look—"

Deacon Ray held up his palms in surrender. "I know what you're going to say." In a voice that mimicked her own, he continued, "There are boundaries in this house."

Okay, now he'd stepped over the line.

"Deacon Ray, that's enough!"

Before she could continue, he reached and pulled her into an embrace. "C'mon, Allie. Lighten up a bit. Remember that time we were underneath the bleachers on the football field, and I kissed you for the first time."

Before she knew what was happening, his mouth was on hers.

"I knew it!"

She pushed Deacon Ray back and turned to find Ryan standing at the doorway. He rushed and put both his arms around their legs. "I knew you two loved each other! We're going to be a family again."

Allie gave Deacon Ray's shoulders another shove. "What? No!" She drew a ragged breath, trying to collect herself. "Deacon Ray, stop!"

Ryan became confused. He teared up.

"Damn it, Deacon Ray! Look what you've done." She cringed. Rarely did she curse, especially in front of her son. Unnerved, she glanced over at Ryan. "Baby, this is not at all what you think. Now, go to your room like I told you and shut the door. Your dad and I need to talk."

He hesitated.

"Now!"

Ryan's chin dropped to his chest. "Yes, ma'am." He trudged out of the kitchen and disappeared down the hall. His bedroom door closed.

Allie took a deep breath, tried to collect herself. "What in the world were you thinking?"

Deacon Ray opened his mouth to answer.

She held up her open hand, stopping him. "Never mind. It doesn't matter." She took several steps back, rubbed the front of her neck. "Look, this isn't working."

Deacon Ray moved for her, tried to take her hand. "Allie—"

She wrenched away. "No, don't start. Nothing you can say is going to change my mind. It's time for you to move out. You have a job now, and well, frankly, you've overstayed your welcome." She looked at him with a forced look of benevolence. "I appreciate you taking an interest in being Ryan's father, really I do. He needs you. I'm not trying to get in the way of that, but this—" She motioned between the two of them. "This isn't working anymore. We are no longer married, Deacon Ray. You've got to go."

He seemed to sense she was serious. He nodded. "No, I get it. And that's all right. I—well, what can I say? I've loved being here with Ryan, Allie. I missed him. I think he missed me. Guess I just—"

She parked her hands on her hips. "This isn't about you and Ryan. It's about you and me. And all this." She swung her arms out wide. "We can't go back, Deacon Ray. I—well, I'm starting a new relationship with Cameron Davis. I'm not sure where our new friendship might lead. Maybe nowhere. But you and I? We can't go back to who we used to be." Her voice took on a softer tone. "You understand, right? You have to go."

Despite his inebriation, or maybe because of it, his eyes filled with emotion. He reached and touched her chin. "Yeah. I guess you're right." He sighed, looked to the ceiling then back at her. "Give me until next week to find a place."

She let out the breath she'd been holding. "I'll give you the weekend." She nervously brought her thumbnail to her teeth, hoping he would stick around like he'd promised. For Ryan's sake.

"Allie?" He ran his fingers through the top of his hair.

"Yeah?"

"Those other women? Well, they didn't mean a thing." He paused. "It was always you I really loved."

She slowly nodded. "Sure, yeah. I know."

24

Allie gathered up her jacket and coffee thermos and made her way through the galley of the boat. Today, their guests included eight former Boise State Bronco football players who gathered every year for a reunion. When one of them hooked a thirty-pound salmon, the guys whooped and hollered like he was sprinting for a touchdown in the last seconds of a playoff game.

"Another great day," she thought wistfully.

The fishing season would be slowing soon. Even now, bookings had dropped, and she'd soon have to go to three days a week. Luckily, business had been strong in these early weeks of fall, allowing her to put a dab of money away. From her calculations, she'd have enough to tide them over through the winter months when revenues would be low.

She had a plan to use the off-season months to focus on getting her captain's license. While Captain Paul was a tremendous asset to her business, he had made it clear he hoped to return to full-time retirement at some point. At the very least, he planned to take his wife on a trip to Europe for their fortieth wedding anniversary late next spring. "If I can get

Darlene away from the Chamber of Commerce," he often bantered.

Allie made her way down the gangway plank, glancing around for her Blazer. Despite her reluctance, she'd lent the car to Deacon Ray. He was moving out today, and while he didn't have a lot of personal belongings, his Harley served as poor transport for anything larger than his duffel bag.

She spotted him waving from across the street and waved back.

At the car, he hurried over and opened the passenger door for her. "Hey, how'd the fishing excursion go?"

"Good." She told him about the football players and their enthusiasm.

He hurried and climbed in on the driver's side, started the ignition. "Sorry I missed it. We could've talked shop. I used to play ball, remember?"

Allie refrained from pointing out that characterizing playing tight end for the Ding Dong Dobermans had very little in common with an NCAA division team. She simply gave him a weak smile. "So, did you get everything moved?"

He started the engine. "I was done by mid-morning."

She frowned. "I thought you said you had a lot to do and needed the car all day."

Deacon Ray pulled onto Bay Street, thumbed the steering wheel to the tune on the radio. "I did." He tilted his head toward the back seat.

Allie turned. "What in the world? What's with all the cases of...beer?"

Her ex-husband grinned. "It's for you!"

"For me? I'm going to drink fourteen cases of beer?"

Deacon Ray didn't try to hide his enthusiasm. "We're having a party—a crab feed. Down at the boat slip. Don't worry. I paid for everything out of my first paycheck. A little thank-you for all you've done for me these past weeks."

She shook her head. "No, that's not necessary. Really." Deacon Ray would throw a party for any reason. "First, I don't have time. Second—"

"I already invited everybody."

She scowled. "Who is everybody?"

Deacon Ray slapped the steering wheel with excitement. "The whole dang town!"

Allie buried her forehead in her hands. How was she going to get out of this one? "Deacon Ray, I appreciate the sentiment. But there are no thanks necessary. I really don't think—"

"You should've seen the excitement on Ryan's face. He helped me plan it all."

Oh, now he was playing dirty. Again.

Her resistance crumbled. "So, when is this little—get-together?"

"Tomorrow." Deacon Ray made a turn at the corner. "Everything's all planned and taken care of. Me and Ryan made sure of that. You won't have to lift a finger. Just enjoy the party!"

THE FOLLOWING AFTERNOON, Allie headed for the docks and the slip that housed *Reel Time*. True to Deacon Ray's word, he had taken care of everything. Partying, it seemed, was one of his rare skill sets.

Multi-colored paper flags and white holiday lights were strung between light poles. The filet tables were cleaned and set up as a temporary kitchen with steaming cooking pots on portable outdoor propane burners stationed just a few feet away. There were borrowed lawn chairs and card tables set up. Coolers spotted the docks, likely filled with beer on ice. Some were marked with handwritten signs that read: *Soda*.

A portable MP3 player had been wired to speakers attached

to the pilings lining the dock along the pier. He'd even attached bunches of helium balloons to the railing of the boat.

Everything looked so festive. A tiny bit of excitement bloomed in her stomach. She hated to admit it, but maybe this get-together would be fun after all.

Deacon Ray rushed over to greet her. Her son followed close on his heels. "So, what do you think?"

"Yeah, Mom. Looks like a real party, huh?"

Allie couldn't help but smile. They'd gone to a lot of effort. "Yeah. Looks really festive. You boys outdid yourselves."

Ryan beamed. "The balloons. Those were my idea."

She drew him into a shoulder hug. "Well, everything is great."

It wasn't long before people started arriving. From the looks of the crowd gathering, it indeed looked like the whole town had been invited. Many she'd never even met yet.

Muncy and Cam were among the first to arrive.

"Looks like quite the celebration," Muncy commented, giving her a peck on the cheek.

Cam nodded in agreement. "Sure does. Now, tell me what Deacon Ray is celebrating again?" He nodded at her ex-husband, who was making his way over.

Allie's face broke into a gentle smirk. "All this—well, apparently, this is his way of showing appreciation for all I've done for him over these past weeks."

"So, this party is for *you*?"

She rubbed the back of her neck. "Yes, Deacon Ray's boat is always filled with great excuses. This time I'm his oarsman."

His arm went around her shoulder. "Well, I'm not one to pass on a good time. Whatever the reason."

"Ah, there you are," Deacon Ray motioned for them to join him. "Cam, I need your help cooking the crab. You up for that?"

Cam and Allie exchanged glances. "Sure." Cam gave her a

little squeeze before letting go. "You know what they say—an apron is just a hero's cape on backwards."

"Yeah," Deacon Ray said. His gaze followed a blue-eyed blonde with a curvy build who smiled at him as she walked by. "Met her this morning at the store," he explained.

Allie rolled her eyes and turned her attention to Cam. "I'll help you," she offered, then followed him as he made his way to the filet station and the waiting pots.

Cam waved over his dad. "C'mon ole man. Make yourself useful."

Together, they opened three large canvas bags teeming with live crabs. Allie had to look the other way when Cam and Muncy dropped the unsuspecting victims into the boiling water, especially when they scratched and clawed the sides of the pot.

Muncy laughed at her. "Crustaceans don't experience pain like we do. Their nervous system is very different from those of vertebrates like us. Scientists believe that since lobsters and crabs don't have the same brain anatomy as we do, that they cannot feel pain. The reaction you are seeing is simply their reflexes. Like when the doctor taps your knee, you flex involuntarily."

Allie nodded but still looked away.

When the first round of crabs had finished cooking, Muncy hollered for people to line up. She and Ryan helped serve.

Deacon Ray was nowhere to be found. Allie suspected the pretty blonde might know exactly where he was.

She hated to admit it, but she was having a good time. It had been forever since she'd helped host a party, and everyone seemed to be enjoying themselves—and they told her so.

There were several customers she recognized from the Pig 'n' Pancake, and Sam Marcum, the cook. Ellen Jeffers from the Whale Museum was there, as was Captain Paul and his wife,

Darlene, who was dressed in cropped white jeans and a cute yellow-and navy-blue nautical-styled top.

Cam's friend, Susan Wilson, the gal who owned the store down on Highway 101, loaded her plate with crabs. "This is the most fun I've had all summer. Thank you for inviting me."

Wylie and Grace Duvall were there. They owned the Pacific Bay Oyster farm she and Cam visited. And, she met a new couple—Olivia and Ben Arrington.

Olivia gave her a warm smile. "I know I'm a bit late with this, but welcome to Pacific Bay. We're really glad you're here." She learned Olivia was an artist—a glassblower who had a little shop behind their house tucked deep in the woods off Highway 101. "I hope you'll drop by and I'll show you around," she offered.

"I'd love that," Allie said while scooping a helping of salad onto her paper plate.

When the line thinned, she insisted that Ryan and Muncy go eat. She helped them fill their plates and watched as they made their way to a couple of empty seats.

She couldn't help but smile as she listened to the music and gazed out at all the people talking and laughing. "I confess, Deacon Ray's plan was a good one. Even if he bailed and didn't help out much." She nudged Cam's shoulder with her own. "Thanks for all your help today. I really appreciate it."

Cam studied her with disarming intensity. "My pleasure."

"Tell me something, Cam."

He carried an empty tray over to the sink area. "Yeah?"

"What kind of husband were you? A good one, I bet."

He shrugged as he rinsed the tray under the hot water faucet. "I don't know that I was so easy to live with. I don't demonstrate everything I feel. I'm stubborn at times. And, I was a little tight about money."

She watched him intently. "Still, sounds like you had a good one, a relationship built on mutual trust and respect. That's valuable, I think." She let her words settle and watched for his reaction.

He shook his head. "Ah, well, good marriages take a lot of work."

Allie let out a chuckle. "I won't argue that. Even bad marriages take effort."

Cam slipped a towel from his shoulder, dried the tray. "I was actually a little surprised to find a woman in love with me."

She tipped her head to one side, looked at him intently. "Why? Don't you like yourself?"

"Yes, I do." He winked. "I just didn't expect it to be contagious."

They shared a smile.

Allie stood, brushed off her palms on the front of her jeans. "Hey, I'll be right back. I'm going to go check on the boat." A lot of people had gathered up on the deck of *Reel Time*. She wanted to make sure all was well.

As she neared the gangway, she heard Deacon Ray's laughter. She made her way to him. "Where have you been? This is *your* party," she reminded. That's when she noticed the half-empty whiskey bottle in his hand.

"The boys wanted something a little stronger," he explained.

She took a deep breath. Nothing would be gained from making a scene. If things got too out of hand, she'd send Cam and Muncy up to throttle his little private party back down to an idle. "Just be careful," she warned, before moving on.

As she proceeded to the bow of the boat, she glanced back. He was making his way down the gangway and toward the beer coolers.

∼

CAM WATCHED as Deacon Ray approached with a smirk across his face. "You sure look good in an apron. You about got all the dishes done?"

Cam looked him over before he nodded slowly. "Yup. Still at it if you might want to lend a hand."

Deacon Ray let out a laugh. "Yeah, right." He pointed to the phone in Cam's front shirt pocket. "Mind taking a picture of me? You can text it to me."

"Where's your phone?"

Deacon Ray pointed to the boat. "Battery ran down. I've got it plugged in to charge." He shifted on his feet. "You and Allie sure seem to have a lot to talk about these days."

Cam tossed the towel over this shoulder, picked up the clean tray. "We like each other's company."

A calculated grin formed on Deacon Ray's face. "You know what I think?' He belched. "I think you're banging Allie."

Cam's jaw turned to stone. He slammed the tray onto the metal surface of the filet table. His eyes narrowed. "Banging. That's kind of an ugly expression for that particular pleasure."

Deacon Ray grinned. He took a step, stumbled. "How about *boinking*?"

Cam shook his head. "Don't like that one much better."

Allie's ex pulled the bottle to his mouth, took a drink and used his sleeve to wipe the sides of his lips.

Cam pointed to the whiskey bottle. "Maybe you've had enough."

Deacon Ray picked up a plate of crab shells and tossed it into the nearby garbage can. "Yeah? Well, I had her first. Probably could have her again."

Cam fought for control. He lifted his chin and rolled up his sleeves. "Like I said, I think you've had enough. If you want to push the point, I'd be happy to plant your face in that bucket of smelly crab shells."

Deacon Ray stepped forward. "Well, is that so?" he challenged.

"You are a miserable SOB, you know that? I don't know why Allie let you in her house. I'd have sent you out to sleep on the dock with the seals." Cam closed in on Deacon Ray. "And I'll tell you something else, you jackhammer." He got within inches of Deacon Ray's face. "Party or no—you're about to get your butt kicked into the Pacific Ocean. You might want to back off before I lose my temper."

Deacon Ray quickly held up his free hand in surrender. He let out a slight chuckle as he waved the bottle with the other. "Man, no need to get testy. I'm only kidding around," he said, his voice wavering. He drew his hand through his hair.

The vein pulsed in Cam's neck as he squared his shoulders. "That's the first intelligent thing you've said."

ALLIE HAD BARELY REACHED the bow of the boat when she felt a hand on her arm. "Allie?"

She turned to find Craig Anthony standing with a bottle of beer in his hand. She hadn't known he was here at the party. Of course, he was Deacon Ray's new boss, so it made sense he was extended an invitation.

"Hello, Craig," she said, her voice a bit wary. Cam didn't care for the guy. In her mind, that was sufficient reason to keep her distance. "Did you get your fill of crab?"

He shook his head. "Not a fan. Of seafood, that is. I'm more of a steak kind of guy."

She nodded. "Well, we have side dishes. And lots of desserts. We don't want you to go hungry."

He held up an open palm. "I'm good. Actually, I was hoping to talk to you about a business proposition."

Allie glanced around, tried to conjure a smile. "I'm not sure this is the time or place."

He failed to look at her. Instead, he focused his attention on the Pacific Bay Bridge in the distance. "I want to make you an offer." He took a swig of beer, then redirected his gaze at her and waited.

She swallowed. "An offer for what?"

Craig slid a sealed envelope from his jacket pocket, handed it to her. "This explains."

She looked at him, puzzled, and took the envelope. Her fingers slid under the seal, and she removed a two-page-stapled document that read *Buy and Sell Agreement*. Her eyes scanned the contents.

"You—you want to buy *Reel Time*?"

"Yes," he confirmed. "At a very generous price, as you can see."

She quickly shook her head. "My boat's not for sale."

He looked at her patiently. "Everything is for sale—under the right circumstances and money."

Allie simply looked at him, not knowing what to say. She was not going to sell Craig Anthony her boat. It was all she had, her only source of revenue. She needed that income to live on. "*Reel Time* is not for sale," she firmly repeated.

From the other side of the boat, a crowd mingled, their chatter drifting from inside the cabin and the deck.

He shot her a meaningful look, lightly touched her wrist with his fingers as if to soften the blow of what was coming. "I've made your crew an employment offer, including Captain Paul." He recited their current salaries, the amount she was paying them dollar-for-dollar. "Like I said, everything is for sale under the right circumstances and money. If they turn down my initial offer, I'll up the compensation package. I'll keep increasing the pot of gold until they fold. Everybody caves eventually." He shrugs. "I plan to repeat the process with any new hires. You might say I have a bottomless bucket of persuasion."

Allie felt a stab of pure fury. "How do you know what my employees are paid?" Then she knew. The open file cabinet in her bedroom.

Her eyes narrowed. "Deacon Ray."

He grinned at her. "That redneck ex-husband of yours—well, let's just say his tailgate is always down."

She found herself unable to answer. Her heart pounded, and she clenched her fists, searching for the right words to put this financial bully in his place.

That's when she first smelled it.

Smoke.

25

"Fire!"

Allie gasped, turned in that direction. Thick gray smoke filtered from one of the open portholes. Her hands went to her chest. "Oh, no!"

Craig saw it too. He grabbed her. "C'mon. We've got to get out of here."

"No, I have to—" She tried to pull away, but he was too strong.

"C'mon," he repeated, his grip firmly pulling her along the outside railing. "Safety first. We have to get everyone off this vessel in case it blows."

"But my boat—" It took a minute to register what was happening as she let herself be pulled along. She was shocked at how thick the smoke was billowing from inside the cabin. The scene was unbelievable.

People on board screamed and ran for the gangplank.

Allie's mind went on auto-pilot, sheer terror driving her. She couldn't think, couldn't assimilate what was happening or the scene playing out in front of her—of guests scrambling for safety, pointing at the smoke.

As they neared the exit ramp, Craig pushed through the crowd to the point of nearly knocking over a guy in a plaid shirt and his wife. He grabbed an extinguisher fastened to the wall and triggered it to no avail. The flames were too much for the effort, valiant as it were.

Allie pulled herself free, took several steps back toward the galley. The crowd continued to scramble down the gangplank and onto the deck. Some pointed. Others held their hands over their mouths in shock.

Suddenly, an explosion rocked the boat, so intense she lost her footing and fell to the deck. Flames shot two feet in the air. The crowd below let out a collective scream.

While brightly colored balloons popped and lay limp, Allie's emotions pulled taut against her chest.

The fire immediately found more fuel. Sparks leaped onto the dock, marring the shiny white surface.

Allie coughed as she got back to her feet, aware someone was trying to beat back the flames with his shirt. The man soon realized he was fighting a losing battle and gave up. He reached for her hand. "It's no use," he said as flames licked the sides of the cabin. She could barely make out the portholes or even the fishing pole rack.

Embers flew everywhere, finding new places to burn, the heat growing more and more intense. For a brief moment, she considered going for the bait box she knew was filled with water, but she had no container. Likely, the effort would make no difference anyway. Not against these flames.

She was shocked and terrified when she saw how much worse the fire had gotten in just minutes. She searched for her phone, pulled it from her jeans pocket, crying. "We have to call 911," she yelled frantically.

The words had no more left her mouth then she heard the sirens. She jumped back from an explosion of new fire.

"Allie!" a familiar voice hollered through the chaos.

Before she could move, another figure appeared—Cam.

He barreled through the smoke toward her. Without hesitation, he scooped her up. "C'mon, we've got to get you off here."

She pressed her face tightly against his chest, admittedly terrified. He scrambled the short distance past sizzling and leaping flames and shot down the gangway with her in tow. The man who had tried to help put out the fire followed close behind.

A fire engine pulled up, and several firemen went into action, shouting orders and pulling a heavy hose across the dock.

Her heart pounded against her chest. Her eyes scanned the gathered crowd. "Where's Ryan," she screamed, her eyes now streaming with tears.

"I'm here, Mom." He rushed to her side, wrapped his little-boy arms around her waist so tight, she nearly couldn't breathe. Except for her son's welcome voice, all she could hear was the crackling flames. *Reel Time* was barely visible now for the smoke.

She coughed.

Despite hose water being shot in that direction, the heat emanating from the edge of the dock was intense. A crash echoed across acrid smoke-filled air as a portion of the boat deck collapsed into the water.

Her gut clenched. The reality of what was happening hit her again. Her skin grew clammy as she watched her beloved *Reel Time* burn.

"Oh, honey." Ellen Jeffers's arm went around her shoulders.

Allie looked upon the tragic scene with disbelief. She sobbed and watched in horror as her uncle's boat—her sole source of revenue, her dream of owning her own business—went up in flames.

26

Allie pulled her old Blazer up in front of her house and parked, turned off the car. She stared at the salvaged burnt remnants of her boat on the floor of the passenger side, the few things she'd asked Cam to retrieve when the fire was finally out—a piece of partially melted silver railing, a fragment of charred porthole frame, a broken spoke from the steering helm. The stench of smoke filled the car. Even so, she wanted these mementos.

She should leave them out on the deck and let the items air out before carrying them inside, she thought. And she needed to look for the insurance papers.

Cam had pressured her not to be without support—to stay at his house. When she'd declined, he'd wanted to come with her. "Then, let me stay with you. You shouldn't be alone."

She'd assured him that wasn't necessary.

Her mind was mangled, and all she wanted was solitude to sort out her thoughts. She'd even left Ryan with her new friends, Olivia and Paul Arrington. "He'll be fine. I'll distract him with a tour of the glass blowing shed," Olivia offered.

Allie was grateful to everyone. The guests, the entire town, had certainly attempted to come alongside and support her in this loss. And while this was not the death of a loved one, it was remarkable how similar it felt to the occasions when she'd lost her parents. Especially the disbelief and sick feeling inside, knowing she couldn't turn back time and make things right again.

How had it come to this?

Only months ago, she'd arrived in Pacific Bay with not much more than her son and a bunch of hope—dreams of starting over, of turning the page on her life and rewriting her story to include a happy ending.

While this turn of events was not the final chapter, the fire had dealt a plot twist she'd never seen coming. It wouldn't be easy to recover.

She remembered the first time she set eyes upon *Reel Time*. Many would have seen a run-down commercial fishing vessel long past its glory days. She saw—ah, she saw all the possibilities.

Perhaps the vessel had technically been seaworthy, but her uncle had allowed her to age, and not so gracefully. The work required to bring the rundown boat up to a standard worthy of competing with the likes of Anthony Charters had consumed many hours and had nearly drained her pocketbook.

In the end, it had all been worth it.

Allie closed her eyes and recalled the first fishing voyage, the excitement she felt inside and the enthusiasm her guests exhibited as they made their way out of Pacific Bay and into the ocean. The shouts when the first fish—a cabezon, if she remembered correctly—was landed.

Her mind drifted to the first time she'd walked into the bank with her very first deposit, how her business account had begun to grow with her careful management of funds.

She glanced over at the items on the floor of her vehicle, and her soul withered.

Now, it was gone—all of it. *Gone.*

Reel Time was nothing more than a charred shell that barely held afloat as water lapped its scorched remains.

She should be grateful no one was hurt, she supposed. There certainly could've been potential injuries, given the explosion. Everyone was safe, and she would be eternally grateful for that blessing.

Still, nothing changed the deep sadness inside her. The insurance policy would pay her a tidy sum, but her limited finances in those early days had forced her to take out a shell policy with a high deductible—one she now had no way of paying. She couldn't rebuild.

Her dream was gone.

The best she could hope for was that she could find a job that would help support her son.

She cringed, remembering Craig Anthony's offer, how Deacon Ray had sold her down the river. Tears stung the backs of her eyes. No matter how much effort she put into changing her life, situations and people seemed to always betray her.

Her mama's voice broke through her thoughts. "Remember, when things take a turn for the worse, simply flip the page. Chances are, you never know what story might be in the very next chapter."

Allie lifted her chin.

Yes, she'd been gut-punched. The waves of this change had left her feeling hollow. Yet somehow, she had to find her way past the fact her boat had burnt down. For her sake—and for Ryan's.

She took a deep breath, glanced at the floorboard, and decided to leave the mementos there for the time being. She'd deal with the items tomorrow. She gathered her purse, pulled the phone from inside. There were texts, lots of them. Offers of help, sincere messages of condolence for the loss of her boat, and encouragement.

There were several from Cam.

"*Let me know if you change your mind about tonight. I can come over. I don't like the fact you are alone right now.*"

Her thumb slid across the face of her phone. "*I'm fine,*" she pecked out on the tiny digital keyboard. "*Let's plan to get together in the morning. You can help me figure out where to go from here.*" She paused, weighing whether to add the sentiment still on her mind. She shrugged off her reservation. Today had taught her not to rely on anything remaining static. Life can change in a moment. She took a deep breath. "*Thank you for being there for me today.*" She hesitated briefly, then added, "*I love you.*"

Allie clicked off her phone and slid it back in her purse as she made her way to the front door. In the streetlight, she could make out flower boxes at the windows overflowing with red and white geraniums. The wooden screen door gleamed with a fresh coat of shellac. This tiny bungalow was home—her home. Despite today's loss, she still had that. She could already feel herself breathing easier.

She pushed her key into the lock and turned, only to discover the door already unlocked.

That's strange. Perhaps she'd forgotten to secure the lock this morning in her hurry to get to the party.

She pushed the door open. Moonlight poured through the windows. She reached and flipped on the light switch—gasped! A knot immediately formed between her shoulders.

Deacon Ray sat on the sofa, his head buried in his hands.

27

"Deacon Ray! What are you doing here?" Allie tossed her purse onto a chair, held up her hands. All the ease she'd felt moments before vanished. "No, never mind. It doesn't matter. I want to be alone. You have to go." She kicked off her shoes.

A loud sob broke across the otherwise still room.

The pained sound startled her, the same as if she'd walked upon a wounded wolf pup in the woods. "Deacon Ray? Are you —crying?"

He looked up then, the expression on his face wrecked.

Still, she couldn't seem to move. It was as if her feet were planted in cement. She simply stared—and waited. The wooden flooring felt cold against her feet, even through the fabric of her socks.

Tears streamed down her ex-husband's face. Allie studied him, struggling to keep her face expressionless.

"I—I'm sorry, Allie. It was me. It was my fault." He sniffed loudly. "I plugged my phone in the battery pack to charge and —and the firemen, well, they said that was where the fire started." He looked up at her, his eyes red and his hair sticking up like a ten-year-old little boy's. "I started that fire."

She supposed she should have erupted into fury. Her body, her emotions, they betrayed her. There was no anger, no need to retaliate. Like an overcooked noodle, she could no longer stand sturdy. She simply slumped into the chair, realized she sat on her purse, and moved it.

"I don't know what you want me to say, Deacon Ray."

"I'm everything he said I was."

"Who?" She rubbed at her temples. Her head was now pounding. All she wanted was to go to bed.

"It's true, Allie. I'm a damn idiot with no brains—a bad person."

She sat, stunned into silence. The remorse in Deacon Ray's voice was the closest thing to humility she'd ever seen in her ex-husband, and it took her a minute to process it.

She struggled to still her shaking as she considered the impact of his statement. He looked like driftwood swirling hopelessly in the middle of the jetty. For good reason, she supposed. Deacon Ray had left a string of mistakes and bad choices in his wake.

"I—I don't deserve you and Ryan. I've failed you both too many times."

Allie stared at him, amazed at his bravery. He'd put into words the thoughts that had run through her own mind far too often. Both she and Ryan had been the victim of Deacon Ray's lifestyle on more occasions than she liked to count.

Still, it wasn't in her to be mean. "People *can* change."

An image appeared in her mind, of a much younger Deacon Ray waiting for her at the end of the aisle. She'd been disappointed to find him not looking at her with adoration. Instead, he was staring wide-eyed at his father, who sat on the front church pew with his beef-like arms crossed against his chest, his eyes dark as a tomb staring back at his son with disapproval.

People said Eldon Barrett was a mean man, especially in his early years. That his wife and son had better toe the line or feel the brunt of his displeasure. Allie remembered once seeing a dark, angry bruise on her mother-in-law's arm. When she'd asked about it, Deacon Ray's mom pulled down her sleeve. "It's nothing, dear," she quickly answered.

Despite her father-in-law's reputation, perhaps well-earned, Deacon Ray adored him and tried everything he could to please the ole cuss. Seemed he never could. Perhaps that was why he simply gave up and became everything his pop expected of him—and despised.

She couldn't pretend to understand it all, but her heart softened, regardless of how angry she felt. The sight of him now standing there, his arms hanging at his sides, tore her apart.

Before she could stop him, Deacon Ray was at her side. His arms tightened around her, clinging to her like a lifeboat. "I'm so sorry," he sobbed against her hair. "For all of it. The women, the unpaid bills, the way I left you alone to raise Ryan." His voice was filled with resigned and profound despair. "Worse, I betrayed you—sold you out to Craig Anthony. And now your boat is gone—it's all my fault. I ruined everything."

She felt the unexpected sting of tears behind her eyes. Did Deacon Ray deserve her forgiveness? Perhaps not.

Her mama always said that harboring resentment was like drinking poison and expecting the person who harmed you to die. For Deacon Ray's sake, and her own even more, she knew she had to forgive him. Even if part of her didn't want to.

She grasped his shaking shoulders, gently pushed him back. "Deacon Ray, look at me."

He focused on her, his face troubled, his eyes tormented. "Yeah?" he managed to say, his voice barely audible.

A realization sunk in. Deacon Ray was indeed a little boy

standing before her—a child in a man's body. He dropped his head, looked downward. Shame seemed to weigh him down.

She was immediately overwhelmed with a terrible sadness, a sense of sorrow that surpassed even the loss of her boat. "Deacon Ray, I have something important to say. I need you to listen carefully."

Wiping his eyes and nose on the back of his hand, her ex sniffed, then raised his head. "I'm listening."

She looked at him long and hard, with nothing but pity. "You did a terrible thing. It doesn't mean you're a terrible person." As soon as she spoke the words, she felt the weight of their truth. She continued, "Remember our first Christmas together? I had never had a real Christmas tree, and you went to the Dallas Zoo and talked them into letting you clean out the monkey pens. You worked all day hauling all the waste from those pens to earn enough money to buy me a spruce, green and pretty, just like in the magazines. I came home from my shift at the diner and you had the tree all set up with lights and everything."

He nodded.

"And that time I had the flu. You held my head over the toilet when I was too weak to even speak. You made chicken soup from scratch and made me eat and drink so I didn't get dehydrated." Her throat tightened with emotion. "You have to decide whether to believe what someone like your father says about you, or what is true. I know it's hard to look at the truth when it runs contrary to what we believe deep inside ourselves. The truth is, you are a good person, Deacon Ray. You just need to live in that truth—make choices that line up with who you really are."

She looked at him with compassion. In that moment, as their eyes met, they both knew she had released him from any penance, any right she had to hold him responsible for all the wrongs.

Deacon Ray let loose a low, keening cry from somewhere deep in his belly. He couldn't speak for several minutes. Finally, he collected himself, put his hand gently on hers. "Thank you, Allie. I mean it."

There may be those who would judge, would say she was a fool to give Deacon Ray a pass after all he'd done. He'd trampled on her love, left her and Ryan on their own, and then showed up and took advantage of her generosity. No one could argue he'd hadn't made a mess of things.

Forgiveness was not a pass; it was an extension of compassion. It was loving someone—valuing a person not for what they do or don't do, but because they mattered.

She closed her eyes, tilted her head back as if gravity could keep her tears at bay. But they seeped out from under her closed lids.

For the first time in many years, she felt as free as a star.

28

llie pushed the heavy glass door open and made her way into the bank. She marched directly to Charlie Truesdale's desk.

He extended his dimpled hand. "Hello, Allie. I was so sorry to hear about your boat. What a bad break."

"Yes, it was," she agreed, taking a seat. "I know you don't have a lot of time, so I'll make this quick. I need to open a savings account."

He straightened his tie. "Oh?"

"Yes, I got the insurance proceeds and want to deposit them." She slid the insurance company's check across the desk in his direction.

It was then she saw a familiar figure walking toward them. She stifled a groan.

Mayor Anthony smiled broadly. "Well, hello again." She reached her hand to shake Allie's. "Good to see you, Ms. Barrett."

She smiled weakly. "Hello, Mayor."

"I was so sorry to hear about the accident. What a terrible loss."

There was a lot Allie wanted to say. She held her tongue. There would be nothing gained from exhibiting her dislike for this woman—and her son. She grimaced and forced a response. "Things happen," she shrugged. "A person just has to move on."

Mayor Anthony pursed her bright red lips. "You don't plan to rebuild?"

"No," Allie admitted. "I'm a— Well, the deductible was rather high, and I simply don't have the funds."

Mayor Anthony's brows shot up. "Not ever?"

Allie rubbed at her forehead, hoping to end this conversation for good. "No, I don't think so."

How could she explain that more than her boat had gone up in flames in the fire? Her dream had been scorched as well. She didn't have the money or the will to dare to dream of starting all over. There was no shame in giving up. She was resilient and this would simply be one more occasion to prove that fact.

Mayor Anthony looked at her with brazen pity. "I'm sorry to hear that."

She wished she believed that. Though thwarted by the fire, her son's well-designed plan to push her out of the business indicated otherwise. She'd even initially suspected his involvement in the fire until the firemen indicated otherwise.

Allie grabbed a white envelope from the rack on the bank manager's desk and dug in her purse for a pen. "Well, nice chatting with you, but I have another appointment," she said, dismissing the mayor and her inauthentic condolences.

She finished making her deposit and darted for the door, glancing up at the security camera before she exited.

If only she had the nerve to stick out her tongue and wag it!

Outside, she made her way down the sidewalk to her car when her phone rang. Cam's name appeared on the screen. She slid her finger across and answered. "Hey, what's up?"

"You've been through a lot this week. I thought I'd take you out tonight for a little fun."

She couldn't help but smile. "A date?"

"Yes. Ryan's included."

"Oh, so not a *real* date," she chided.

She could hear Cam chuckle. "Well, I plan to kiss you good night. So... I call it a date."

"Okay." She laughed. "I give. We'll call it a date. So, where are we going?"

"It's a surprise. Be ready at six?"

She stopped walking. "Wait! What do I wear?"

"Clothes."

"I know that, silly. I mean, do I dress in jeans or a dress?"

He hesitated briefly. "Casual is fine."

Later, when she told Ryan they were going to spend the evening with Cam, he didn't seem surprised.

"Do you know something I don't?" She bent and picked up the football off his bedroom floor. "What does Cam have cooked up?" She handed him the ball, eyeing him for clues.

Ryan could barely suppress his grin. "Nothing," he said, in a manner that did little to convince her he wasn't in on some idea to buoy her spirits. "We—I mean, he doesn't have anything special planned."

Allie raised her eyebrows, rubbed the top of her son's hair. "Well, sure. If you say so." She knew that look. Cam definitely had something going on, and Ryan was in on it.

Cam arrived promptly at the planned time. He leaned and kissed her lightly on the cheek. "Hope you're ready for some fun."

Grabbing a lightweight sweater from the back of the chair, she followed him out to the car. "Thanks for getting me out of the house, Cam. I—well, I've been fighting slipping into the dumps." She told him about her trip to the bank and her encounter with the mayor. "I don't know how she can look me in the eyes knowing what her son tried to pull—would've pulled had the boat not burned."

Cam nodded as he opened the car door for her. "There's a saying—what goes 'round comes 'round. Seldom does a rotten seed produce a fruit tree, know what I mean?"

"Yes, I do know." She glanced to the back seat where Ryan clicked on his seatbelt. She lowered her voice. "I've decided to let a lot of things go. None of this is worth my mental energy."

Catching her off guard, Cam reached and took her by the chin, tilted her face to him. "I understand not dwelling on the ills in life. But it's okay to be angry. About all of it. I know I am." He released her chin, patted her leg. "But you're right. Anger can be a dark emotion that will drain you if you let it. I'm proud of the way you are picking yourself up and moving on."

She clicked her own seatbelt. "Moving on. That's me."

Ryan piped up from the backseat. "Mom's not going to have any trouble being happy tonight. Is she, Cam?"

She saw Cam wink at her boy in the rearview mirror.

Allie narrowed her eyes. "I don't know what the two of you are up to, what kind of fun you have planned." She clapped her hands enthusiastically. "But I'm all in."

Cam made the short drive to Main Street, pulled to the curb in front of the movie theatre and cut the engine.

She climbed from the car and noticed a crowd gathering across the street. "What's going on over there?"

Cam followed where she was looking. "Oh, there's an auction over at the Legion Hall."

Her eyes lit up. "Auction? What are they auctioning?"

Ryan's eyes lit up. "Lot's of stuff. Right, Cam?" He nudged him with his elbow.

Playing along with their not-so-well-hidden surprise, she put her hand on Cam's arm. "So, is that where we're going tonight?"

He smiled back at her. "Well, I donated a few pieces of my art, so I'm betting we might. C'mon."

Inside the Legion Hall, the place was packed. A taxidermy moose head was mounted on the far side wall next to a series of framed oil paintings of ships out to sea. In the corner, a pole in a stand held the U.S. flag. Rows of tables covered with red-and-white-checked oilcloth were crowded with people bent over looking at items.

There were handmade quilts, mason jars full of canned vegetables and little jars of jam and preserves. Packages of beef jerky crowded the space with hand-carved wooden spoons and letter openers. Spinning racks were filled with handmade earrings, some made with shells. Necklaces and matching bracelets hung from a rack.

Another table was loaded with freshly baked cookies and pies, cakes mounded high with frosting. Next to the table was an open space with large numbers taped to the floor.

Across the room were racks of clothes hanging, all tagged with handwritten prices. Several women milled around examining the garments and nodding their approval.

In the front of the room, a large man with a wide smile sat behind a podium with a microphone. The wall behind him held a flasher board with numbers lit up.

Allie stood with her mouth open, taking it all in. She glanced between Cam and her son. "Wow. This is quite the deal."

A woman with white tightly curled hair and wearing a dress with a tulip design at the hem sat with her shoulders straight, her frail hands tightly gripping the handle of a small ping-pong type paddle painted with a number. She glanced at Allie and gave her an odd wink.

A man Allie didn't recognize took the podium up front. He had a rotund belly and wore red suspenders. He leaned into the microphone, cleared his throat. "Okay, everyone. We're ready to bid on the next item. The woman by his side held up a beautiful lamp with the base made out of shells. "This lamp was donated by Deac Peterson. Handmade."

An audible murmur floated across the room as the people stopped to appreciate the item. Many held paddles with numbers.

The little woman with the tightly curled hair looked over the top of her glasses. She quickly raised her paddle high in the air. "Fifty dollars," she belted out in a voice that did not match her diminutive stature.

"Okay, we have a starting bid of fifty dollars," the man at the microphone repeated for the crowd.

A man several feet away raised his paddle. "Sixty."

Allie grabbed Cam's arm. "I want to bid!"

Ryan grinned. "Me too! Am I old enough?"

"Sorry, son." Cam pointed to a sign on the wall that said you had to be eighteen. Upon seeing the disappointed look on her son's face, he pulled a roll of candy out of his jacket pocket and handed it over. "But you can go get in the cake walk." He nodded in the direction of the area where numbers were attached to the floor. He dug in his wallet and handed Ryan a twenty. "Try and get the one loaded with coconut."

Ryan's eyes widened with excitement. "You bet!" He raced off, barely bothering to look behind him.

Allie followed Cam to a table in the back of the room, one of the only tables with space left. Several people greeted them on the way, each giving her a wide smile.

There was Candy Paulson, the bank clerk, and Bill Reynolds from the hardware store. The Duvalls and the Arringtons waved. As did Susan Wilson and Sam Marcum. Even Captain Paul and his wife, Darlene, were sitting at a table with bingo cards before them. There were nearly as many townfolk here as were at the party the day of the fateful fire.

Cam pulled out a rickety folding chair for her, then sat

down beside her. An attendant quickly made his way over with numbered paddles. "That'll be four dollars each." He winked at Cam.

Quickly dismissing the puzzling gesture, Allie leaned over her paddle and studied the number. "How do you bid?"

Cam picked up his paddle. "Just raise the paddle high and yell out your bid. I warn you, it can get a little chaotic. These people mean business. From the looks of this crowd, the bids could be fairly large this evening. The Legion Hall does things a little differently. On top of the winning prizes, some successful bids will also net you a freshly baked cake or a dozen homemade maple bars, thanks to the Thelma Kennedy." He pointed up front. "She records all the bids and takes the money."

The man at the microphone called out, "Paddles ready?" He nodded to Thelma.

She held up a beautiful painting. "This is by one of our local artists, Cam Davis. As you can see, it's an image of the lighthouse out on the point."

"Starting bids?" the man at the podium bellowed into the microphone.

Allie bit her lip. She didn't have a lot of cash to spare, but she wanted that painting. Sure, Cam could always paint her another, but she found herself caught up in the moment and desperately wanted to win. "Twenty dollars," she said loudly while lifting her paddle high above her head.

"Fifty," came a voice behind her.

"Seventy-five," said a woman at the back of the room.

"One-hundred-fifty," said that dratted little lady with the curls.

Allie pulled her paddle down and placed it on her lap. The bidding had surpassed her cash reserves.

"Going once—twice—SOLD!" the man at the podium bellowed.

The little lady with the curly hair stood and did a little victory dance.

Over the course of the next couple of hours many more items were auctioned off, often in sets and packages. Each time something was offered, the bidding quickly escalated to amounts that made Allie shake her head. Deflated, she kept the paddle in her lap.

"Okay, the final item for the evening is donated by the Duvalls. He held up a huge wire basket of oysters. "Oysters pulled fresh this morning and all the fixings." He pointed to a box filled with lemons and bottles of hot sauce. There were containers of baked beans and potato salad, all packed with tiny bags of dry ice.

A thin man wearing a Pacific Seafood cap hollered, "Two-hundred dollars!" He looked around as if daring anyone to bid against him. When no one raised their paddles, he grinned expectantly and turned his eyes to the man at the podium.

Two attendants hurried over to his side carrying the basket of oysters and the box of food.

The man at the front nodded. "Looks like we have a winner. Mr. Lewis, you won a nice dinner there."

The man who won lifted clasped hands in a victory wave.

A man sitting next to him gave him a congratulatory slap on the back. "You can finally give poor Edith a break and fix *her* dinner...even if out on the BBQ."

The winner shook his head and winked. "You got that right. Got to keep the little lady happy."

The man at the front announced a five-minute break and reminded everyone the bar was open at the back. "For those old enough," he reminded. "And those not driving tonight."

Allie and Cam checked on Ryan over at the cake walk. Upon seeing them, her son rushed to their side holding an enormous chocolate cake. "Sorry, Cam. The coconut one went too fast. But I got us this gorgeous baby." He proudly held the massive dessert up for inspection. "Mom, this is so great. You just walk around the numbers until the music stops. If you're on the winning number, you get to pick out a cake to take home."

She ruffled his hair. "Glad you're having a good time, sweetheart."

Allie excused herself and made her way to the restroom. Minutes later, she came out of her stall to find a woman leaning into the mirror, putting on lipstick.

"Well hello, Allie." Ellen Jeffers put the cap back on the tube and slid it into her bag.

Allie flipped the water faucet on and drew her hands under the running water. "Hey, Ellen."

"I was afraid I wasn't going to be able to get away from the Whale Museum in time for the auction tonight. There are always those few tourists who won't seem to call it a day, know what I mean?" The middle-aged woman gave her a warm smile. "So, are you having fun?"

Allie finished drying her hands. "Oh, yes. I've never played been to an auction before. It's really a kick."

Ellen straightened, checked her hair one last time in the mirror. She looked at her watch. "Well, I suppose it's time we can get back in there." She moved for the door. Allie followed.

Cam looked up from a small table when she slid into a chair next to him. "There you are," he told her. "Thought maybe you'd ran off with the guy and the oysters."

"Sorry," she apologized. "I bumped into Ellen, and we talked for a minute."

"Oh, yeah? What did you talk about?" Cam slid a Dr Pepper in front of her. "I took the liberty."

"Thanks." She marked the center spots with her dauber. "Nothing really. We just chatted."

"Ah," he said, marking his cards. He smiled over at Ryan.

Ryan winked back before turning his attention back to her.

"Mom, can I go get a candy bar? There's a bunch of girls selling some back at that table." He pointed. "I have enough money left over."

She glanced between the two of them, then nodded at her son. "Yeah, sure. Just come right back."

"So, what's with all the looks and winks between you two?" she asked Cam.

He directed his attention to the paddle on the table before him. "What? Nothing, why?"

Before she could respond, Thelma Kennedy cleared her throat from the front of the room. She gave the microphone a few hard taps. "Well, we have a grand total raised tonight." She leaned forward, clearly excited. She reported the amount and beamed.

Cheers went up from across the room. A few people patted each other on the back.

Allie took a deep breath, leaned over toward Cam. "Wow! I had no idea that kind of revenue could be raised." She loved that about small towns, and particularly Pacific Bay. Everyone supported good causes. She'd heard the library had been built and funded entirely through donations.

She looked across at Cam, bumped his shoulder. "Well, should we go? Looks like everyone is leaving and heading out."

He nodded. "You bet."

Allie waved Ryan over and they followed Cam to the door. She couldn't help but think about how things had changed. There were times over the days when she'd been more depressed than she wanted to admit. Who packs up a tiny trailer behind an old Chevy Blazer and treks across half the country with her kid to move into a house she'd never seen? Little did she know she would meet someone as amazing as the man sitting next to her. And she never expected to live in a community of such caring and wonderful people. Even though she'd run into bad luck with the fire, and all, there was something to be said about living in a community of caring people. She was not alone.

Allie glanced over at her son and Cam, sharing a soda and laughing at something she wasn't privy to. Cam's eyes found hers over the rim of the can. He smiled.

She remembered how Cam's dad had given her a job when her bank account had whittled to less than the cost of a tank of gasoline—how Cam had helped her find a captain for *Reel Chances*. He'd been there at every turn, ready to put her unsteady feet on sturdy ground.

Here's the thing—if she was going to make a life for herself and for Ryan here in Pacific Bay, she'd need every friend she could get. Cameron Davis was a good one.

Her thoughts wobbled a bit as she considered once again what it might mean to go beyond casual dating to something serious. If she were honest—she was ready for more. She'd even said those three little words—*I love you*—over the telephone.

That thought brought a half-smile as they headed out the door and into the dark night air.

Outside, they crossed the street. That's when she saw them —all the people from inside the hall had somehow made their way out the side door and had gathered on the sidewalk. And more. Even Mayor Anthony and Craig stood in the crowd.

Each one of them lifted a lit candle in the dark. Two boys she recognized from the grocery story held up a big sign that read:

We love you, Allie.

She rubbed her eyes, blinked several times. "What is all this?"

"Surprise, Mom!" Ryan nearly exploded with excitement. "It's for you!"

Confusion flooded as her hand went to her mouth. "I—I don't understand."

She saw Deacon Ray standing to the side of the crowd, next to Muncy. He gave her a timid wave. She smiled back at him.

Cam pulled her into a shoulder hug. "The residents of Pacific Bay all felt so terribly bad when *Reel Time* burnt. We suffered the loss with you. The way we figured, it made sense that we shared in helping to make things right."

"What?" Tears sprouted. "I don't understand." But she did. They had orchestrated everything—had gone to such lengths for organize this auction event. For *her*. She could use the money, and they knew it.

Captain Paul stepped forward and handed her an envelope. "Open it," he said.

"Yes, open the envelope," his wife, Darlene, urged. "It's from all of us."

With shaking hands, Allie slid her finger under the seal and pulled the flap open. Inside was a check written in an amount that far exceeded what she thought she needed to fix the boat. She could hardly believe her eyes!

"This—what? This is too much!" Incredulous, she looked at Cam, tears now streaming down her cheeks. "I can't accept this."

"Of course, you can," he assured her. "We all want you to have it. Now you can cover the deductible. You can replace *Reel Time*."

The impact of the news hit her. She nearly crumbled with gratitude. "I can't believe this. I—I don't know what to say."

"Just say you'll throw another party when you christen your new boat!" Muncy shouted.

Allie breathed in the salty air, heady with joy. She wiped the tears with the back of her hand. "It'll be my absolute pleasure!"

29

Allie climbed from the Blazer, her arms loaded with groceries and items for the big boat christening party. She was going to throw a party like this town had never seen, far surpassing the one Deacon Ray planned on the night of the fire. Because of their generosity, she'd been able to meet the deductible and rebuild her boat in record time.

The process had been all-consuming, with lots of decisions. Thankfully, she'd been guided in the process by Captain Paul and Cam, and many others. So many knowledgeable people had stepped up and helped. She had to hire a maritime engineer and a company who could frame and do the build-out of the structure. She had to choose a new engine, hire painters and welders. The Coast Guard had to inspect the final product and issue a new license.

The endeavor had taken months, but here she was at the end of the arduous journey. Not only was she excited to celebrate with everyone, but she had a bit of a surprise. Not even Cam knew of her last-minute decision.

Overhead, gulls cawed as they darted to the deck leading to her front door, landing only feet away from where she stood.

"Oh, no. This bread is not for you," she told them. "If you want to chow down on anything in these bags, you'll just have to fly over to the boat docks and grab party leftovers."

She laughed as one of the gulls stomped its webbed feet and launched in the air, not bothering to look back. The other birds followed.

A sputtering engine noise caught her attention. She turned as a truck that had seen better days pulled up and parked. The bed of the extended cab pickup was loaded, the items covered with a blue tarp and secured with knotted ropes. Inside was a young girl with blonde hair. She gave a timid wave.

In the driver's side sat—*Deacon Ray*?

Allie quickly placed her grocery bags inside the front door and moved to further survey the situation.

Deacon Ray climbed from the car. "Hey, Allie," he said with an impish grin. "I wanted you to meet somebody." He pointed to the girl. "This here's Linda Lowry. Linda's a friend of mine from Seattle." He rubbed the back of his neck before rushing to open the passenger door.

The girl who climbed out didn't look a day over twenty-one. Puzzled, Allie extended her hand. "Nice to meet you."

Deacon Ray shuffled his feet before pointing to the back. Allie leaned over and peered in the window. She gasped.

There were two car seats with two young toddlers. One had sticky Tootsie Roll in his hand.

She went wide-eyed as she looked at Deacon Ray. "What's this?"

Her ex-husband pressed his hands deep inside his back jean pockets. "Surprise! This is Peter and Patrick. Linda says they're mine." Rushing on, he added, "It's kind of funny. I keep getting boys."

Allie swallowed, trying to take in the information. Stunned, her hand went to her chest. "Well, congratulations?" Attempting to cover her shock, she turned to Linda. "All the way from Seattle, huh? That's a long way to drive with two little ones."

"Yes, ma'am."

"Well, come on inside." Allie placed her hand at her throat and rubbed. Deacon Ray was a package that came with many surprises. Even so, she'd never seen this one coming. She extended a gracious smile. "Uh, we're having a party down at the docks this afternoon. You're welcome to join us." She gazed at Deacon Ray. "All of you."

"Can't, Allie. We're heading out." Deacon Ray dug in his pocket, pulled out a house key and offered it up to her. "We're going to have to get on the road if we're to make it up to Seattle before dark. Can't really afford a motel."

She took her key. "You're leaving?"

Deacon Ray nodded. "Yeah. I wanted to say goodbye. And I wanted to explain everything to Ryan before I go."

Allie scratched behind her ear. "Yeah. He'll want to say goodbye." Her heart sank at the mixed news. His leaving would create a vacuum in her son's life, but she was glad Deacon Ray was stepping up to his responsibility.

Allie stared at Linda, trying to comprehend how a girl could be so gullible. Then it dawned on her. She'd been that girl several years back.

Allie drew a deep breath. Well, at least Deacon Ray likes kids, she thought. And he'd promised to turn over a new leaf. Time would tell whether he was serious and intended to live his life differently. No one could force him to change. He had to want it from deep within himself.

Allie pointed to one of the babies. "Do you mind?"

Linda shook her head. "No, of course. Go ahead."

Allie opened the car door and brushed her hand through one of the toddler's soft hair. She remembered clearly when Ryan was that age, remembered how soft his skin was and how she used to run her fingers across the dimples in his hands.

Deacon Ray placed his hands on his hips. "I know what you're thinking, Allie."

"Yeah? What's that?"

"I'm not going to mess this up," he promised. As if to prove what he was saying was true, he pulled a check out of his wallet and held it up for her inspection.

Her eyes widened. "Where'd you get all that money?"

"Now don't go looking at me with all that suspicion. I sold the Harley. I plan to sign a lease on a nice place, put some of it in a college fund for the boys—all three of them."

Allie saw Ryan approaching. "He's home."

Deacon Ray looked at them. "Let me, Allie. I need to be the one to tell him."

She reluctantly nodded. "Okay."

She watched as Deacon Ray joined Ryan, placed his arm around his shoulders. After listening to his dad, Ryan nodded his understanding.

Allie folded her arms against her chest. She was unsure how Ryan would take the news that his dad was leaving. No doubt, he would be hurt.

After a few minutes, the two of them made their way back to the house. Deacon Ray led Ryan to the car seats. "These are your half-brothers, Ryan. This one here is Peter." Deacon Ray pointed to the second little guy, patted his chubby knees. "And this is Patrick." He smiled at Ryan. "You can hold 'em if you want."

Ryan looked back at Allie. She nodded.

Deacon Ray introduced Linda, and they unstrapped the toddlers. Ryan alternated holding them.

He grinned. "They are kind of cute, aren't they, Mom?"

"Yes. They are cute."

Allie stood pondering how she felt about all this. Deacon Ray had surprised her. He'd sold his prized motorcycle. He'd made a commitment to help raise the tiny boys.

She leaned over and whispered in his ear. "You plan on marrying her?"

"Who, Linda?"

Allie rolled her eyes. "Yes, Linda."

"Well, sure. These boys need parents who are committed—to them and to each other." His face broke into a silly smile. "It's time I made some of those good choices. Do it right this time."

Allie couldn't help herself. She reached and drew him into a hug. "Well, I'm proud of you, Deacon Ray."

When she pulled back, she noticed his eyes had grown a bit misty. "I'll miss you," he told her.

At the truck, Deacon Ray handed an envelope to Ryan. "Inside is the hundred dollars I borrowed," he explained. "And a little extra. Maybe next summer, you can come up and visit us for a few weeks. We'll be making frequent trips back to Pacific Bay to see you too. I promise."

He helped strap the boys in and opened the passenger door, waited for Linda to climb in before he shut the door.

He turned, and their eyes met. Her ex-husband leaned and brushed her cheek with a light kiss, then whispered, "Thank you, Allie. For everything."

30

Allie arrived at the boat docks to find Cam and many of their friends standing side-by-side making preparations for the big celebration. Unlike the party Deacon Ray had put together, the party that ended in the eventful fire, this affair had an air of distinctive charm.

There were linen-covered tables lined with wine bottles and glasses, platters with cheese and deli meats cut paper-thin and rolled up. A four-piece string quartet was setting up and delicate floral arrangements in pots graced the wooden planks leading to the newly built boat. A crane was positioned with a large hook fastened to a massive canvas tarp standing ready to pull for the big reveal.

She was a bit scared at how untethered she felt. Not only was she fighting a major case of nerves, but Deacon Ray's leaving had left her feeling a bit adrift. Something deep inside told her that chapter of her life was indeed closed, as it should be. She needed time to adjust.

"There you are," Cam exclaimed when he saw her. He rushed over. "How do you like how everything's coming together?"

"It's lovely," she told him. "Really beautiful."

She told him about her morning and about Deacon Ray.

He shook his head. "Well, honestly? I can't say I'm sorry about that." He wrapped his arms around her. She could feel his newfound appreciation that they were on the other side of the situation. "How did Ryan take it?"

"He's strangely okay with it. Of course, he was a little excited at the thought of having half-brothers."

"Does he realize it's going to be quite a while before those twins are old enough to play ball with him?"

They smiled in agreement as Cam leaned in closer, kissing her on the forehead. As he did, his phone rang. He ignored it, but she could feel his body tense.

"Aren't you going to answer it?"

He shrugged, pulled his phone to his ear.

"Who is it?" she mouthed.

"Yes, Mayor Anthony. We're glad you and Craig are joining us." He paused, listened. "Yes, uh-huh. We'll see you then." He clicked the phone off, pushed it back into his pants pocket.

"The mayor is coming? And Craig?" A sense of dread quickly rushed over her. "But why?" It was the last thing she wanted.

Cam was quick to assure her everything would be okay. "Seems the residents of Pacific Bay have figured out that Mayor Anthony and her son were only going to have as much power as was handed to them. They collectively made a decision that they are done handing them any. She was given the clear indication that they were ready to pull funds out of her bank and that she didn't stand a chance of being re-elected next fall if they didn't back off their attempts to thwart your new business."

Allie teared up. "You're kidding?"

Cam grinned back at her. "Nope. They gave an ultimatum. Seems Mayor Anthony caved, and she passed her newfound commitment to make you feel welcome onto her son. They won't be bothering you anymore."

A catering truck pulled up. Two men in white aprons got out. "Where do you want us to set up the food?" they asked Cam.

She looked at him with amazement. "You're kidding, right? More food?"

"We're doing this party up right," he told her, then motioned for the caterers to follow him.

Allie looked up to see Olivia Arrington moving toward her. She was dressed in a pretty ankle-length blue dress. Her long hair was casually fastened up on her head. "Hey girl," she said and drew her into a hug. "Ben will be here later. He had some work he needed to finish up at the aquarium." She paused. "I saw Deacon Ray down at the gas station."

Their eyes met. "Oh? So, you also saw his new family?"

Olivia's face broke into a tiny smile. "I did."

Allie shrugged and smiled at her new friend. "Diaper flipped backwards spells *Repaid*." They walked toward the festivities where others were now gathering. "Kind of poetic, don't you think?"

"I do," her friend agreed.

When everyone had eaten, Cam reached for her hand. "It's time."

She let him lead her to a designated place on the dock. "Could we have everyone's attention?" The entire party semi-circled around them. "Allie has something she wants to say."

Allie stepped forward, tiny beads of sweat breaking out on her brow. She wasn't one to love the stage, but there were sentiments she needed to convey.

"Everyone, thank you for being here. More, thank you for opening this community and your hearts to me and my son. You've gone out of your way to make us feel welcome and we appreciate that more than words can express."

To the side of the crowd stood Mayor Anthony and Craig. They both smiled at her warmly, perhaps a little disingenuous, but smiles none the less.

She went on. "Many of you knew my Uncle Tarver. This was his home, and because of his extreme generosity, and yours, Pacific Bay is now our home as well."

She looked over at the attendees, cleared her throat. "Not so long ago, I thought I'd lost any hope of moving forward with a commercial fishing boat business. Few tourists want to board a burnt-out shell of a boat to catch their ocean haul or go whale watching. But it seems the good Lord, with the help of many of you saintly people, had the audacious idea of allowing me to restore Uncle Tarver's boat with your generosity."

She turned, gave the signal to the man in the crane. He started the engine and maneuvered the levers until the giant hook began to rise, lifting the boat cover.

"My mama always said, 'Chances are, you never know what story might be in the very next chapter.' I've certainly found that to be true, especially here in Pacific Bay. So, I've decided it's appropriate to christen the new boat with a new name."

The cover lifted off the boat. In the sunlight, lettering gleamed from the starboard side. "The name of our newly rebuilt boat is—" She paused for effect. *"Chances Are."*

Applause went up from the crowd.

Allie clasped her hands over her heart. "I love you all, from the bottom of my heart." She looked over the excited crowd of people. "Now, get yourselves another glass of wine. And dance!"

The music started up.

Cam moved to her, with Ryan close on his heels. "Well done," he said.

"Yeah, Mom. You did cool."

She ruffled her son's hair. "You think so, huh?"

He looked at her wide-eyed. "Can I go get some more ice cream?"

She smiled. "Sure."

He raced off and joined a group of his friends at a table where Muncy was scooping large helpings of ice cream into bowls.

Cam turned to her, drew his finger tenderly along the line of her chin. "You know something? I was incredibly lucky to be deeply in love once. Now, surprisingly, I'm in love again."

She dared to stare into his eyes. "I'm in love for the *first* time."

He kissed her then, full on the mouth. A kiss filled with longing. She grabbed his shirt, wrenching him close to her and devouring his mouth with her own.

When they finally pulled back, wetness welled in her eyes as Allie contemplated her past, her beautiful future. She took a breath, smiled. She was ready to get started.

With the beginning of it. The next chapter of her new life.

ALSO BY KELLIE COATES GILBERT

THE PACIFIC BAY SERIES

Chances Are

Remember Us

Chasing Wind

Between Rains

THE SUN VALLEY SERIES

Sisters

Heartbeats

Changes

Promises

LOVE ON VACATION SERIES

Otherwise Engaged

All Fore Love

TEXAS GOLD SERIES

A Woman of Fortune

Where Rivers Part

A Reason to Stay

What Matters Most

ABOUT THE AUTHOR

Kellie Coates Gilbert has won readers' hearts with her compelling and highly emotional stories about women and the relationships that define their lives. A former legal investigator, Kellie's deep understanding of human nature is woven into every page.

In addition to garnering hundreds of five-star reviews, Kellie has been described by RT Book Reviews as a "deft, crisp storyteller." Her books were featured as Barnes & Noble Top Shelf Picks and were included on Library Journal's Best Book List of 2014.

Born and raised near Sun Valley, Idaho, Kellie now lives with her husband of over thirty-five years in Dallas, where she spends most days by her pool drinking sweet tea and writing the stories of her heart.

www.kelliecoatesgilbert.com

SNEAK PEAK - REMEMBER US

Chapter 1

On the morning of her thirty-sixth birthday, as on every morning, Olivia Arrington woke before dawn. Careful not to disturb Ben, she climbed out of bed, dressed in her running clothes, pulled her long hair into a ponytail, and headed outside into the foggy Oregon morning.

Their small house was located a couple of miles north of the tiny coastal town of Pacific Bay, off Highway 101 at the end of a long gravel lane tucked deep in the woods.

When she and Ben had first seen the house, it had been a beautiful sunlit July day. They'd been out driving, enjoying their time together after an afternoon crab feed at the home of some friends. While they hadn't been looking to buy a house, the for-sale sign stuck alongside the road piqued her interest.

"I thought we decided to wait until we had a down payment saved up," Ben argued, when she begged him to go venture a look.

"Please, let's just check it out," she urged.

They drove down a winding lane lined with pine trees to find a quaint little two-story farmhouse in need of love, a sagging wraparound porch, and three acres filled with ferns and blackberry bushes. A span of green grass surrounded the house, bordered by towering pines, mostly Douglas firs, but a few Spruce. Naturalized flower gardens filled with roses, hydrangeas, dahlias and azaleas lined the lawn and the winding path that led deeper into the woods. The clearing at the back especially drew her in. "Look, Ben! That's the perfect spot for my glass studio." She pointed. "We could put a tiny parking lot for visitors over there and a small vegetable garden on the other side, with a composting station."

It was Olivia's dream, her slice of paradise. She loved the secluded location, the fact their home would be only visible to those who bothered to find it. Ben, on the other hand, felt differently. "We live in one of the best coastal communities in Oregon, Liv. Why are we not building where we can see the ocean?"

In the end, he'd given into her wishes, as was often the case. They both knew she could be stubborn. He didn't want to battle over what he considered the small things.

The first thing they did to the property was gut the inside, leaving the original wood flooring scarred by decades of wear and the ceiling beams in place. They installed massive windows that overlooked the lush green surroundings. Together, they picked out cabinetry and furnishings. Using the small inheritance from her deceased grandparents, she hired an architect to design their living space. The leftover funds had gone toward building her small studio in the lot out back. And, they made a small clearing that gave them the perfect view of the ocean in the distance, right from their front porch.

When the projects were finished, she'd slipped her arms around her husband's neck. "Thank you, Baby. This is everything I ever dreamed of."

Ben scooped her up into his arms, laughing. "No problem," he told her, as he climbed the stairs to their bedroom. "Just so you know, the bill just came due and it's time to pay up!"

Ben was one of the good ones. Everyone in town said so.

Damp air chilled Olivia's face as she squinted into the misty darkness. She jogged along the narrow, twisting, tree-enshrouded lane, and for the hundredth time thought about how much she loved living by the ocean.

While a vacation at the beach was known to temporarily reduce stress levels, people who lived near the ocean experienced this same benefit on a daily basis. Running along the shoreline calmed her soul like nothing else.

Olivia paused at the highway, looked both ways before proceeding across the pavement and down the opposite side, a steep slope leading to the beach. When she reached the sand, she stopped and bent over to catch her breath.

A moment later, she straightened and took off again, determined not to waste her time alone on the beach.

She'd inhaled this scene hundreds of times, yet it never got old—the way the sky looked at dawn, the hint of pink that ran along the water in the distance, the gentle roar of waves crashing onto the packed shoreline, the smell of salt air mingled with the pungent aroma of seaweed cascading across the wet sand.

She picked up speed, pushed herself. Soon, she felt her heart rate increase, could almost sense blood coursing through her veins at a rapid pulse. It was at times like these she felt most alive. Maybe the only times.

It certainly hadn't always been that way. In the not so distant past, she was different. She could easily embrace life, all of it. The highs, the lows, and everything in between. She wasn't constantly filled with a tiny sense of dread.

That was before.

She continued her run, listening to her running shoes hit the sand in a rhythm that calmed her.

As the sky lightened, she bent to pick up a broken sand dollar, lifting it carefully from the wet sand and examining its fragility. Sand dollars were made of durable calcium carbonate plates with textured spines meant to house sea echinoids. Unfortunately, this shell's strength had succumbed to a blow it hadn't seen coming. Some would think it marred. She saw a thing of beauty and tucked the broken shell inside her pocket to add to her garden collection.

Olivia glanced at her watch, realized it was time to turn around and head back. With a deep sigh, she reversed direction and ran as hard and fast as her feet would take her, ignoring the burning in her lungs.

At the house, she entered through the side door leading into the kitchen. Ben sat at the table perched behind the newspaper. "You're back," he said, without looking up.

"Yeah." She untied the scarf from her neck and flung it over the back of a chair before moving for the coffee pot. She turned, scowled in his direction. "It's empty."

He pulled the paper down. "What?"

"The coffee pot. It's empty." Seeing the blank look on her husband's face, she simply shrugged. "Never mind."

Ben went back to reading the paper and she moved for the cupboard, flung it open with a little more force than she intended. The cupboard door banged.

"Hey, take it easy. Those hinges aren't made of steel."

She set her jaw. "Last I looked, they were made of metal."

"Not the point." He positioned the paper back in place.

Olivia pulled the canister down off the shelf, carefully measured out two and a half scoops of her favorite French roast blend. She carried the carafe to the sink and filled it with water. "Have you eaten?"

"I'll stop and grab something at the Pig 'n' Pancake." He

folded the paper and reached for the remote, turned on the television. He always checked the weather before heading out.

Ben brought his coffee cup to his mouth, paused as he heard the weather man announce the date. He took a deep breath, looked over at her. "It's your birthday."

"Um-hmm," she replied absently. She turned the coffee pot switch to on, then gathered the paper, folded it and headed for the porch. She placed it on the stack. When she returned, Ben was standing. He studied her for a moment, his dark eyes narrowing to seek out the place where she couldn't hide from him. She didn't know whether to blush or be annoyed. "Yeah?"

Ben crossed the floor to join her. He reached for her hand, brought it to his mouth and gently kissed her knuckle. "Look, it's your birthday. Let's celebrate. We could pack a picnic, head out to Otter Crest and do some whale watching. Liv, remember when we—"

Olivia pulled her hand away. "I—I don't think so." Seeing the disappointed look on her husband's face, she hurried to add, "Besides, today's the day Allie Barrett is dropping her son off."

Ben's face turned dark. "Sure. No problem." He picked up his coffee mug from the table, tossed the remaining contents into the sink. "For the life of me, I can't figure where you thought it was a good idea to keep that boy."

"Allie's a friend. She needed someone to look after him while she's away on a trip with Cameron Davis."

He smirked. "Yeah, some couples like each other. Some actually want to spend time together."

Before she could answer, her husband grabbed his jacket and headed for the door. "Don't know when I'll be home tonight." The door slammed behind him.

Olivia watched through the window as her husband stomped to his truck.

Her lip quivered.

Careful Ben, she thought. *Our hinges aren't made of steel.*

ORDER YOUR COPY OF REMEMBER US NOW!

Made in the USA
Monee, IL
02 July 2021